THE JOURNEY OF MOSES AND POLARIS

DAVID MENDELSOHN

ISBN: 1530854636
ISBN 13: 9781530854639

Novels by David Mendelsohn include:
The Seven Swords of ISIS.
The Message

Cover by Cheryl Suitor. Berryville, VA.

PREFACE

God assigned to Moses a very difficult task. Moses had help along his journey, such as Aaron, Miriam, Joshua and others, and of course, God. However the scribes, who recorded the oral history, omitted one very important helper. They thought he was unimportant, yet we know that for centuries shepherds have had dogs and often, sharing long hours on a lonely hillside with their dog, strong comraderies developed. Yes, the average dog owner is very fond of their pet and hunters boast about theirs. One might say there is no noting in the scrolls that Moses had a dog, yet there is nothing to indicate he did not. No proof existed, until now.....

PROLOGUE

The market place in Cairo was a jumble of stalls along narrow streets. The variety of colors, merchandise and food was impressive. A thirteen year old boy approached one of the vendors and knelt to kiss the man's hands and cheeks, I watched then asked this man if he was a holy man.

He chuckled. "No, that is my nephew and he shows respect. Perhaps there is something here you would like to purchase. My prices are the lowest in all of Cairo."

I looked around. There were carvings of camels and palm trees, t-shirts with a wide array of messages, vases, than a beat up cedar box got my attention. It was what was in the box that intrigued me. Fraying rolls of parchment.

"I see that has caught your eye." He shrewdly stated. "My price is low for such an heirloom."

I asked how he had obtained it.

"A Bedouin discovered this in a cave on the side of a mountain. It is very old. I purchased it from him and it was costly but I shall give you a good price."

I asked what was on the rolls of parchment.

"It's an ancient language, Aramaic, which I cannot read."

I could see he was mentally increasing the price with every question I had and every bit of my continued interest. The parchment looked like it might crumble into dust if I touched it.

Probably worthless, I thought. The box was falling apart also. My wife would have a fit if I brought this back, so I decided against it and started to leave. The vendor called me back and said we could work out a good price so I would be satisfied. He asked for five hundred dollars.

"Very valuable, sir. A lost treasure."

Could be, but probably nothing. Nevertheless I was intrigued. We settled on one hundred dollars, and yes, my wife let me know she thought I had lost my mind.

Back in the United States I had a friend, who teaches Hebrew at the local university, look at the box. He would not touch the parchment for fear it would disintegrate.

We brought it to an expert he knew who took the box and parchments and told me he would take them to his laboratory and look them over when he had time. Four months later he called.

"You won't believe this!" he excitedly screamed.

"What did you find?"

He then told me and this is the story.

CHAPTER 1

I was comfortable, lying in the shade in front of the tent. My tail flicked an occasional fly away.

A few trees were able to survive in this rocky, sandy, too hot and then too cold environment.

The desert stretched for miles. In the distance was another mountain range. Our tent was on an almost level side of a big hill in the foothills of Mount Horeb. There was a stream that ran down the mountain through our hill forming a small pond, when there was rain, but for now the stream bed was dry. My coat was a lustrous tawny, nose black, and I had a joyous attitude.

I had a cool bowl of water and was happily munching on a yummy bone. I yawned. Life was good. I heard a commotion. It was faint but my dog super hearing picked up the sounds. Some people were arguing and I heard my parents angrily barking. I gave a warning bark and jumped up running to the aid of my parents. My people, in the tent, had not heard the noise but they heard my warning bark. Now they were starting to leave the tent and look around for any danger. I was running towards the noise and barking as ferociously as I could. I'm just a pup but I am ferocious and to be feared. I hope.

Mom and Dad were big sheep-herding dogs. They had to be big and tough to fight off any marauding wolves. I heard my older brothers and sisters barking and running towards my parents. What could the danger be?

I rounded a turn of the hill and saw a disturbance at the watering well. . My people's daughters had brought their sheep to water at the well.

I saw several men, other shepherds trying to take the water for their sheep, pushing away my people and their sheep.

When the stream was dry the people had to pull up a sheepskin bag down the well. It would hold water and it would get very heavy. They would pour the water into a wooden trough where the sheep and goats would drink. It took a lot of bags to fill up the trough. My women had done all the work, pulling up the water bags and filling the trough. Now these other shepherds were pushing our sheep away and pushing around our women, even knocking them to the ground.

A stranger, a man I did not know, was now standing between the two groups, my people's daughters, all seven of them, and the aggressive men. He had raised his arms to the sides to separate the men, from our people, and protected the women by this gesture.

He was sun and wind burned and appeared exhausted, but was still protecting the women.

His clothing was torn and his skin showed the ravages of exposure to the sand storms of the desert. He was tall, well built and had a conspicuous black beard.

The men could have pushed him aside easily, he looked to be so weak. But my parents were on the side of the hill, right behind this man, growling with their teeth bared. The rest of the pack, my older brothers and sisters, stood right next to my parents, also growling. I ran right to the front of the pack ready to attack. I was small, only a pup, but I could be a whirlwind of ferocity and strike like a bolt from the sky.

The men saw me standing there in front of the pack, right behind the stranger. I was too much for them. They turned and left.

The man helped the people water our sheep then he took a drink himself. He drank a lot. He must have been very, very thirsty. My parents herded the sheep back to their grazing field and stood guard. The women thanked him for his help.

"Those men were doing evil and I had to stop them," he answered. "If good men do nothing we let evil win."

I snickered. He actually thought he had chased away those men. It was us, the pack.

The women were telling him how he was so brave and strong.

"It was your pack of brave dogs that really stopped those men," the man replied.

"So he knew it" I thought.

"Come with us to our father's tent. You'll eat and rest and tell us how you came to be here," they implored.

The man hesitated, uncertain, while the women ran ahead, quickly out of sight.

I barked, "Follow me", but he didn't understand. I barked again and pulled at his robe. He patted my head and followed me to the tent.

My parent's human, Jethro, was waiting by the entrance to the tent as the group approached.

Jethro was considered to be a wealthy man. He had large herds of sheep and goats. He was a Priest of Midian, a leader among the people.

Zipporah, his daughter, the leader of the women, a raven haired woman of exceptional beauty, told him what had occurred and the bravery of this stranger.

She didn't say a word about me. Grrrrr.

"He must stay here and be our guest." Jethro ordered. "Come in and have refreshments."

"Maybe I'll get some extra morsels too, for it was my bravery and ferocity that did the trick" I thought.

He asked the stranger his name and the reply was "Moses".

"There was something special about this man. He had spirit, integrity and a sense of fair play.

But there was more. I sensed a special destiny he was to fulfill. I decided I would make him my human."

Mom had come back to the tent after the sheep were calmed down.

"Mom, he followed me to the tent. Can I keep him?"

"Hmmm. Yes, it's time you got your own human and learned how to take care of him. It will give you a sense of responsibility."

The people sat down to eat and drink.

"Tell us how you came to be here Moses," Jethro inquired.

I saw that Moses expected the women to serve him as if he was royalty. I barked my "No" bark. It was a deep barking sound. He didn't understand. I barked again and pulled his arm down.

He thought and seemed to recognize my command. He stopped giving orders to the servers.

"I have hopes for him," I thought.

I thought about a name. I know they called him Moses, but that was people talk. Because of his princely bearing and manners I decided I would call him "Prince". Prince was tall, had muscular arms and shoulders a firm jaw and a neat black beard. I guess to humans he was handsome, especially the way the women kept staring and smiling at him.

I had an impressive tan coat with white markings and a very cute face. My ears were cutely floppy. I had excellent vision and hearing. All told I was the perfect dog. Modest too. Oh, my name is Polaris.

So Prince started to tell his story. It was an amazing tale. Not like my tail, which I like to wag. This tale was an account of his life.

"I was born of Hebrew parents but the Pharaoh had ordered all male Hebrew babies to be killed."

The women gasped. "Why would he do such a horrible thing?

"He believed the Hebrew people were becoming so numerous they might be a threat to the Egyptian people. My mother put me in a woven basket and gently placed the basket into the Nile River. She had tears in her eyes as she sent me floating down the river. My sister, Miriam, ran along the river bank watching me. A crocodile nudged the basket and Miriam looked on in horror, but the crocodile turned away. I drifted along into a quiet pool of water where a group of maidens were bathing. They saw the basket and lifted me out. One of the maidens was the Pharaoh's daughter, a Princess who said she would raise this baby as her own. I was hungry needing milk but she had none. Miriam was watching, ran forward, and told the princess she knew a woman who was able to provide milk. The woman was in fact my real mother, Jocahbed. For two years my real mother breast fed me, then I stayed with the princess, who had lifted me from the Nile, my adoptive Mother, in the palace, as a Prince of Egypt."

"Wow", I thought. "I really picked the right name, Prince, for my human."

Moses continued. "As a young man I was a general for the Pharaoh's army. I was honored for bravery and life was good. Everything changed. One day I saw a taskmaster whipping a Hebrew slave and he would have killed him. I was outraged and confronted the taskmaster who raised his whip to strike me. I blocked his whip and struck with all my strength with my fist. He fell backwards over a railing and plunged twenty feet to the rocky surface below, and he died. I should not have hit him so hard but I lost my temper. I regretted it right away but my feeling bad about what I did could not bring him back to life.

His relatives would have killed me, as Egyptian laws allowed, so I had to leave immediately. I left with the clothing I wore taking only a flagon of water. I walked for several days. The water soon was gone, the desert winds and sandstorm tore my clothing, burned my skin, and food was scarce. I caught and ate one lizard which sustained me until I arrived at your well. The rest you know."

The humans sat quietly, absorbing his story.

Finally Jethro spoke. "That's an amazing tale but hard to believe. I see you in rags yet you claim to be a prince. Yet you have courage and a sense of justice. I'm not sure I believe you, yet you are welcome to remain with us. A good strong man will certainly help prevent those men from chasing my daughters from our well."

The man, Moses, thought about it and again hesitated.

I pulled at the sleeve of his robe and gave my 'Yes" bark. It was a higher pitch short bark. The man smiled and seemed to understand.

"Yes," he replied. "I appreciate your offer and in truth have no place else to go. I shall be happy to stay and work here."

I barked my happy bark and the woman gave out shrieks of joy. Jethro had a broad smile on his face and the two men shook hands sealing their agreement.

The man looked at me and said, "I guess you've decided to adopt me. But I need a name for you. I'll call you Polaris, the name of the North Star. The North Star is a faithful, steady point in the sky that travelers and sailors have always used as a guide to determine their location and direction. You guided me to Jethro's tent and I realized you have been guiding my actions and direction since. So you are Polaris."

I was amazed. Polaris was my real name, my dog name. How weird that Prince had given me the same name.

CHAPTER 2

The next year was good. Prince and I went to the fields to shepherd the goats and sheep. He knew nothing about being a shepherd. I had to teach him everything. He gradually understood my "No" bark and my "Yes" bark, and it took time but he started to respond to my other commands, to "come" and to "stay." If he was leading the sheep to the wrong spot I would bark and direct him to the correct path. The goats tended to find their own way. The grasses and shrubs were sparse on the side of the hill so I would bring the sheep to a meadow where they would graze. We sat with the sun warming us in the cold weather or we would sit under the shade of a tree when it was hot. I enjoyed the birds chirping and the blue sky above. The birds also were good watchers and would chirp loudly when intruders appeared, such as a wolf, fox, or strange men. Sometimes a sheep would get himself stuck behind some rocks, or in a stream. They are not very smart animals, not like dogs.

One afternoon I heard a lamb bleating, crying out for its mother. Prince and I followed the sounds and we saw the lamb. It had squeezed onto a very narrow shelf of rock, with a twenty foot drop if it fell off, to get to a bright yellow flower with luscious large green leaves around it. The shelf was too narrow for the lamb to turn around, too high up to jump down, and there was no way to climb up. Prince tied a rope to a tree above the lamb and tied the other end around his waist. As I barked directions to him he climbed over the edge and down the rope. He was next to the lamb and the silly animal was frightened and started to kick. Prince got to the side of the lamb, holding onto the rope with one hand and grabbing the lamb around its midsection with his other arm. I was hoping the rope was strong enough so it would not break. He then pulled himself and the lamb up and shoved the lamb to level ground, and then he climbed onto the level ground. We both were relieved and panting from the exertion but then, would you believe, that silly lamb ran right back onto the narrow ledge to get to another flower. Prince had to climb down again.

"You silly lamb!" he yelled, "I should drop you off this cliff to teach you a lesson."

I barked a warning top him. "No Prince! Control your temper. Remember what happened in Egypt because you lost your temper and hit that taskmaster."

"I know", he said. "I wasn't really going to drop the lamb."

Again he climbed up to safety with the lamb but this time I chased the lamb away from the edge of the cliff, all the way back to his mother, and I growled a warning to the two of them.

Prince was indeed a good choice and I was proud of myself for picking him to be my human. He was a quick learner and after a few weeks knew what to do without my barking at him.

He also spent a lot of time with Zipporah. They would talk for hours, sitting by the campfire in the evening. Sometimes I saw that they would cuddle together at night under the sheepskins.

Jethro knew of this and spoke to him about his daughter, Zipporah. Moses and Zipporah married and had a son, Gershom. Zipporah had adopted the religion of her husband and their son, Gershom, was circumcised. Moses had explained that circumcision was commanded by God to Abraham as a covenant between God and the descendants of Abraham. When Eliezer, their second son was born, he also was circumcised.

I had also done my own cuddling with a cute female dog named, Felicia. She had wandered away from a passing caravan and joined our group. She had a black coat with some spots that were tan and white.

Felicia also worked with us in watching and guiding the flock of sheep and goats.

Now I'm proud to say that while Zipporah gave birth to only two, Felicia, with my help, gave birth to seven. Seven puppies. I wanted to just number them, like Number One, Number Two, but Felicia insisted we give them each a name, and she did, but I still called them by number. Two of the pups had tawny coats, two were tan, two black and one was tan with areas of yellow, white and black. The pups grew.

They learned how to be sheepherding dogs, and were a comfort to us. My parents were getting too old to go out with the flocks and I and Felicia were the now the big dogs of the family.

Grazing sheep and goats devoured the vegetation in the fields down to the roots so we had to always move them to another location. One day, Prince and I, brought the flock to graze on the side of Mount Horeb. It was said that the Creator, called God by the humans, lived on this mountain. The sheep were happily munching when we saw a bush on fire. In this dry climate a fire would quickly spread. Leaving Felicia and the pups, all seven, Prince and I hurried to the burning bush. He was going to douse the fire with water and I would spray what I could. As we got closer to the bush I saw the bush was not burning but rather glowing with a very bright light. I moved forward to sniff the bush and light when I heard a loud, deep voice commanding, "Remove your sandals for you stand on holy ground!" It was the voice of the Creator.

"I don't have sandals," I barked, "only my paws."

"Not you!" the voice proclaimed. "Moses, remove your sandals! Polaris, lie down!"

I was filled with a sense of excitement and joy. The Creator knew my name. I lay down immediately and tried to be still but my tail was wagging furiously.

I looked at Prince and saw that he was filled with awe. He was not afraid but out of respect did not want to look onto the face of God. He removed his sandals and lay prone on the ground. He was trembling, not from fear but from a sense of wonder and admiration at being in the presence of his God.

To hear that voice was both exhilarating and frightening at the same time.

"I am the God of your father, the God of Abraham, the God of Isaac, the God of Jacob.

I have heard the pleas of my people in Egypt, crying for help because of their sufferings," the voice said, "and I will send you Moses, to Egypt, to free my people and lead them from Egypt to the Promised Land. Your task shall be difficult and not without pain and hardships."

After God called Prince by his name, Moses, I decided I also shall call him by that name from now on.

Moses it shall be. It kind of tickled my tongue to say Moses.

Moses was very apprehensive. "Why me, God? Who am I that Pharaoh would listen to me?"

"I shall be with you and shall show Pharaoh signs that you speak for God. You shall not be alone for I am sending Polaris to help you on your journey."

Moses was still troubled.

"Take your staff and throw it to the ground" and Moses did as God directed and the staff turned into a serpent and Moses grabbed the serpent by the tail, as God directed, and it became again a staff.

Moses was astounded but still very apprehensive and voiced his fears but God was persuasive and finally Moses agreed to follow Gods commands, stating, "as you wish so it shall be."

Moses and I started back down the mountain.

I looked at him. His face was determined and he strode with confidence. His beard and the hair on his head had turned white. He had a glow about him and I realized it was from the glow of the burning bush. Some of it had passed to Moses.

"Am I glowing too?" I asked.

Moses looked me over. "Yes, a little on your nose and on your tail. Like bright lights."

I wagged my tail and saw that it created an arc of glowing light and sparks that flew about. That's fun to do, I thought. I wagged some more and started chasing the sparks. Wait, I thought. I'm not a puppy to be chasing my own tail. I'm a mature, proud, fearless dog. I looked but stopped chasing the sparks.

I called to us my pups Three, Five and Seven. "Moses and I must go on a long journey. I am entrusting the care and protection of the flock to you three." As Moses met with Ziporah, his wife, and his sons to inform them and ready them to join with him on this quest, I also met with Felicia and pups One, Two, Four and Six. "You pups must care for and protect your mother, the humans and help in the care of the sheep and goats.

Some people are dreamers and have wonderful ideas but never fulfill them. God recognized that Moses is a doer, a person that strives until the task has been completed. Moses will not give up and neither will I.

"How come your nose and tail are glowing like a bright star?" pup number Two inquired.

"That's so I can help guide Moses and the people."

"But how come they're glowing?" all four pups wanted to know.

"God made them glow."

"How?" they all barked.

"I don't know how God works. God's ways are mysterious. I wagged my tail and the pups joyfully chased the scattering sparks. Now say your goodbyes until I see you again."

It was sad leaving the ones I loved but I was thrilled about the task ahead.

CHAPTER 3

I explained to the pups that the desert can be a very dangerous place. The sun glows with a strong hot fire and there is dry land, little water and little food. You must carry the essentials you will need to survive, such as water, food, blankets, and feed for the animals.

"Is the glow from the sun like the glow from the bush?" the pups asked.

"No, the glow from the bush was Gods special light. There is no light anywhere like that."

"If it's so hot in the desert why do you need blankets?" they asked.

Patiently I explained that at night, without the heat from the sun, it becomes very cold. The humans need blankets to keep warm and sometimes even a dog needs to get under a blanket to warm up.

Finally they had no more questions.

Jethro expressed his fears for Moses, Zipporah and the two boys.

"It's dangerous for you, Zipporah and the children," Jethro worried.

"No fear, God will provide protection." Moses replied.

Jethro sent out some scouts and learned that a very large caravan heading to Egypt would be passing by the next day.

"Looks like your God is protecting you. You are fortunate that you can join a large caravan where there are so many men that bandits will dare not attack." Jethro mused. "It is rare to have a caravan, and one so large, at this time of the year."

"Yes, God is protecting us by providing a caravan." Moses said.

Moses got one camel ready for the trip. He attached four large water bags and hoped the water would last. Bags containing our food were also slung over the camel's back. He also fixed two slings to hang from each side of the saddle. One was to hold a prize sheep that he was bringing to Pharaoh. The second sling was for me. Uh oh, I didn't like that idea. I growled my displeasure but Moses said it was for the best. The desert sand would be hot and hurt my paws and he was also fearful that I would not be able to keep up. I disagreed but finally said I would try out the sling. Moses also readied a donkey to carry Zipporah and their sons and four water bags, food for the humans, for me, and for the camel and donkeys and other supplies were also packed onto a second donkey.

And so it began.

We started at dawn and soon met the caravan as Jethro had informed us. We were Moses, one sheep and one fantastic dog, me, on the lead camel, with a rope attached to a donkey carrying Zipporah and sons, and a rope attached to a second donkey carrying supplies. Moses greeted the caravan master who welcomed us and assigned us to take up the rear. The desert was a land of many small rocks, sandy, poor soil, yet scrub brush grew here and there. Large sand dunes loomed nearby, created by strong winds, blowing the sand into valleys and large hills. It was hot. No shade as we moved along.

I didn't like the rear. The dust kicked up by the camels and donkeys in front of us stung our eyes and made it difficult to breathe. As Moses was higher up on the camel the dust was not as bad for him as it was for Zipporah. Moses held back his camel and we would follow the caravan at a distance so the dust would settle and not be as bothersome. The boys complained and wanted to move up the front of the caravan but Moses explained it was only fair and just that late arrivals would be at the rear.

The sling was not working for me. You have to picture it. My front and rear legs hung down and my body was supported by the sling. I was bouncing and bumping into the side of the camel who didn't want me there anymore than I wanted to be there. Every once in a while, after a particularly rough bump, the camel would turn his head and spit at me. I growled but there was not anything I could do. My tummy was getting rubbed raw. The sheep was hanging from the sling on the other side of the camel. She kept bleating her complaints too. I barked my unhappy bark and Moses understood and stopped. We discussed it and Moses agreed to let me run alongside. He also took down the sheep and tied it on a tether to the saddle of the second donkey so the sheep could walk behind the donkey.

I was very happy to be out of that sling. The sheep however didn't like walking behind the donkey.

You just can't please everyone.

So we continued and it was better. I was free to run back and forth. Moses did not want to get too far behind the caravan and did not want to stop and wait for me. He was not happy that I would stop and sniff the camel and donkey droppings. When I stopped Moses pulled up the camel.

"You'll fall behind and become lost."

I told him I would run and quickly catch up.

"Why must you sniff all this doo-doo?" he asked in an annoyed tone.

"It's instinctive." I replied.

"Yes, in stinky." He laughed.

"Let me explain. Your children are taught history and geography. Dogs however learn history and geography by sniffing. We come from hunters and needed to know where the animals we hunted had been and where they were likely to go. One sniff and we know what part of the woodlands they came from and were likely to return too. We know friends from foes by sniffing. We learn where the good food and water is. It's like a Google system for dogs, if Google was invented then."

Despite these little differences, we kept up, had enough water for us and the donkeys, enough food, and were warm at night. The camels, fortunately, had filled up with water before the trip and with their reservoir of water they can last for several days without the need to replenish.

Once we saw a group of bandits on horseback but with the large numbers in our caravan and me, a ferocious super-fighting dog, they rode away and did not attack.

It took about one week and we were nearing Pharaoh's capital in Egypt when to our surprise a man, waiting in an oasis under the shade of a Tamarisk tree, waved and hailed us as we approached. I had explored the area on and around my mountain but had not travelled the desert and was surprised to find a lush area of shrubs and trees surrounding a tranquil pond of blue water. Moses explained that there is water deep under the dessert and it comes to the surface in some locations enabling grasses, reeds, shrubs and trees to grow and desert animals to come and drink. However sometimes the oasis dries up then everything around it also dies until the water comes back.

The man knew Moses by name and was very eager and happy to see him. It turned out to be Moses' brother, Aaron. It had been years but they knew one another and Moses was overjoyed. They hugged and both did a kind of dance, jumping around, arms raised, singing something, while I barked happily and circled around them. Zipporah laughed and joined in and Moses's two sons, Gershom and Eliezer, stood in amazement as never had they seen their father dancing, then with giggles and laughter they also joined in. It was a happy moment. However there were serious times ahead.

The others in the caravan looked on in amusement and continued their journey.

The caravan master called out to Moses. "Are you coming? It is dangerous to be alone here."

"No thank you." He replied. "Thanks for your help and concern. We are good."

We watched the caravan disappear into the desert.

Moses and Aaron shared some of the water and Aaron brought out some wine and delicacies. The adults enjoyed the wine and food and the children especially enjoyed the delicacies. .Moses let Gershom taste a sip of the wine. Gershom made a sour face and spit it out.

:"How can you drink ,that?" he asked.

Moses and Aaron laughed and Zipporah hugged Gershom.

Aaron had come out on foot, to meet Moses. He had dreamed that Moses was coming. .

He told us. "A dream that he knew God had planted in his mind."

I barked in my quizzical way, pointing to Aaron. Moses understood.

"I'll ask him." He said. "Polaris wondered how you were able to get away from building Pharaoh's city? He thought Hebrews were all slaves. He wondered if you had called in sick, that is if telephones had been invented.

"What's a telephone?" Aaron wondered. "And do you speak Dog?"

"God allowed me to visualize into the future but it is too complicated to explain a telephone.

Polaris and I have been together a long time. We seem able to understand each other."

Aaron told Moses that the sons of Levi, the priests, are exempt from regular work and the Pharaoh respected that. They knew the priests were selected to do the work of God. It was the custom among all peoples to let the wise ones teach their ways. The Egyptians did not want to offend any of the Gods.

Zipporah now urged them to catch up with the caravan for their protection but Moses held up his hand, asking for patience, stating that they were protected.

"How are we protected?" she asked, "There are just you two men, one woman and the children!"

"Grrrrr!" I barked. "Don't forget one ferocious dog."

"God is protecting us." Moses simply replied. "Now let us proceed."

And so they continued to, Aaron riding on the camel behind Moses, until they arrived at the village of the Hebrews. What would happen to them now?

CHAPTER 4

We arrived at the Aaron's home in the village of Goshen. It was small. They had built the hut using a muddy mix of sand, grasses and reeds, poured into a wooden frame, which when hardened formed building blocks. The blocks were stacked one on top of another, using the same muddy mix between blocks to cement them into strong walls. The roof was constructed of wooden poles with bundles of reeds tied on top. There were openings on top of the walls for air to circulate and heat to escape. A small fire pit for cooking and heating, during very cold nights, was in one corner of the room used as a kitchen. There were just two rooms. Sheepskins were spread on the floor to lie upon at night. They had a small area behind the hut where they grew some vegetables. Also a shed next to the house where they kept a few goats and sheep. They used the goats for milking and made goat cheese. The wool from the sheep was used to knit into their clothing. Being the priest for the Israelites Aaron received gifts from the people, sometimes a baby goat, sometimes some lumber or sometimes a grateful family would labor at Aaron's home, so Aaron had a bit larger home and more than the others. Nevertheless this small home already contained Aaron, his wife, Eliseba and their four children, Nadah, Abihu, Eleazer and Ithamer. Now the five of us, Moses, his wife Zipporah, their two sons, Gershom and Eliezer, and of course, Me, were crowding into their home. The open spaces above the walls helped fresh air circulate but even so with all the sweaty humans crowded together and the odors from cooking there was an unpleasant aroma in the hut.

Aaron showed Moses a corner in the room used as a kitchen where his family could lay down their bedding for sleep.

I looked around. "Where's the place for me? The bestest doggie ever."

"Your dog can sleep in the shed with the other animals." Aaron said.

"Grrrrr!" I responded with my definitely NO growl.

"He thinks he's in charge." Moses told the others.

"I am!" But they did not understand my barks.

To my embarrassment they expected me to sleep in the shed with the goats and sheep. How humiliating. They did not have pets. I guess they did not have enough food for pets as it seemed they just had maybe enough for themselves. They did just not understand the greatness of dogs. I decided I would rise above the small humiliation and go along with the flow. To complain and whine would make me appear needy and a pest and I am certainly none of those.

There were two goats and two sheep in the shed. We added one camel and two donkeys. The shed was made with upright wooden poles and reeds attached across the poles to form walls. The roof was the same material, poles and bundles of reeds. The floor was the sandy soil of the dessert, which fortunately absorbed some of the liquid waste from these animals. Dog gone it! They peed on the ground. When I said dog gone it, I wasn't going anywhere. It was just an expression of my frustration.

There was also a lot of straw, dried up grasses, on the ground and I learned that Abihu, Aaron's son, would sweep these out every morning and replace them with fresh straw.

All the children had to work. Ithamer worked along with the other adult slaves pushing, straining and hauling the building blocks into place. Eleazer helped his father in his priestly duties.

Abihu, age 6, cleaned the shed then would go out and gather reeds, donkey and camel droppings, or bits of branches for fuel for their fire pit. Nedab, age 4, helped Abihu. It was dangerous to gather the reeds, which grew alongside the Nile, as crocodiles hid in these reeds and would occasionally snatch an unwary child. When Abihu and Nedab reached ten years of age they would join with Ithamer and the other slaves struggling to build the cities of Pharaoh. It was hot dirty work, with muscles pushed to their limit, little food or water, those who grew weak would pass out from exhaustion or sun stroke and always the whip. No wonder they had been pleading with God to rescue and free them.

I was very uncomfortable in the shed. I had to get out and get some fresh air. The moon was full, shining brightly through the palm trees, creating strange shadows on the ground. It was dark, an area new to me, and it seemed mysterious. I sniffed the air and picked up a familiar scent, that of another dog. Yes, there in the shadows was a big black dog. I approached him and we circled each other and made our hellos.

He was friendly and we chatted for quite a while. I learned some very interesting information. It seems the Egyptians loved dogs and treated them with great respect. They in fact worshipped Dog Gods. The oldest dog god was named Anubis and was believed to guide the departed souls of Egyptians to the underworld, their heaven. Another god dog was, Wepawet, whose image was sewn on Pharaoh's flag. Set and Osiris were also dog gods and Sirius, the Dog Star, guided travelers at night.

Dogs are treated as family members, are well fed and sleep on the softest cushions. Egyptians fear angering a dog as this might mean they would never be guided to the afterlife when they died, that their souls would forlornly wander the earth forever.

I knew it. Dogs rule!

The next day we would go to meet the Pharaoh and I knew what I must do.

CHAPTER 5

As the suns' rays began to shine through the openings in the shed, and the spaces in the hut, I was up barking, making sure we were all awake. We had a quick breakfast. My mother used to tell me breakfast was a very important meal as it gave you the energy needed to start the day.

Moses, Aaron, and I, had some goat's cheese and milk. The goats had straw to eat. They seemed to enjoy it. I would not like to eat straw.

"You're bringing the dog?" questioned Aaron, in a surprised and annoyed tone. "The Egyptians won't let him in!"

I barked and stood proud with my head held high.

"He says you don't know about Egyptians and dogs. They'll love him." Moses replied.

I wagged my tail and shook my head, yes!

First we met with the elders of the various Israelite tribes and told them that God had sent Moses to obtain their freedom. Eldan, the oldest elder was doubtful and asked, "Why should we believe and trust you?"

"Watch" Moses replied. He handed Aaron the staff and it was thrown to the ground where it turned into a snake. Aaron grabbed the snake by the tail, as God had instructed, and it turned back into a staff. The elders gasped and made oohing sounds.

"That's a trick," one of them yelled.

Aaron then put his hand inside his robe and when he took it out his hand was red, swollen, blotchy and twisted with a scary disease, Leprosy.

The elders moved back, not wanting to become infected also.

Aaron then put his hand back into his robe and when he brought it out it was normal.

The elders moved in closer and murmured with "more oohs.

"Still could be a trick." One again yelled, but not too loudly this time.

Aaron then took some water from the Nile River and poured it on the ground. The water on the ground turned as red as blood.

The elders said, "You are sent by God and may God go with you, guide you and protect you.."

CHAPTER 6

We proceeded to the Pharaoh's palace.

On we went, the three of us. Moses carried the staff as instructed by God. The palace guards were not going to let Moses and Aaron enter. I hid behind Moses robe.

"Be gone, slaves!" the guards commanded. "You dare to think you would be allowed to approach the all- powerful Pharaoh? You?" They laughed at the ridiculousness of Moses' request.

"Imagine." One said to the other. "Slaves trying to have an audience with the mighty Pharaoh."

I bounded forward and stood defiantly next to Moses and Aaron. I glared at the guards.

They looked confused and fearful.

"We have no quarrel with you, son of Anubis. As these men are with you all may enter."

We were permitted to pass through the gates and enter a long passageway.

"Told you so." I snickered.

We walked along the long corridor with marble statues on each side. One of the statues was a dog, Anubis, the dog God. Pharaoh's personal guards saw Moses and Aaron approaching and blocked their path.

"Please allow us to meet with the mighty Pharaoh." Aaron requested.

"Are slaves daring to seek audience with the Pharaoh?" They mocked Aaron and laughed at him until I stepped forward from again concealing myself behind Moses robe.

The guard's demeanor changed rapidly. They grew pale and stuttered.

"We do not intend to offend the son of Anubis or Osiris. You may all pass."

Aaron was puzzled. He did not know about dog Gods. Moses remembered though, as he was taught about the many Gods worshipped by the Egyptians, having been raised with them.

They entered Pharaoh's court and there he was.

Pharaoh looked down from his throne. He wore a robe, made of fine linen, embroidered with a colorful design and with strings of beads. On his feet he had leather sandals dyed a bright red. A cape around his head and neck was also embroidered with a colorful striped pattern. A chain of gold hung around his neck with a large medallion resting on his chest.

I was surprised that he had red hair.

"Slaves, less worthy than mere mortals, dare not speak to the Pharaoh." He saw me and instructed his aide to get a bowl of water for me.

I'm special, I thought. Okay, I got you guys in, now it's up to you and God.

Moses, who had always a fear of speaking before others found that God gave him the courage and words to reply.

"We speak to you not as ourselves but for the God of Israel. God desires that you release the Israelites from bondage and allow them to go free!"

"Another God? There are so many of them but I know of no such God of Israel." Pharaoh thundered. "As a child you were raised among us, yet now you are ungrateful. To release the slaves would lead to great hardships for the Egyptian people. No Moses! For your impudence the foremen and taskmasters shall no longer provide the reeds and straw needed to make the bricks but the slaves must complete the same amount of work as before. Go now!"

We left and were very sad. We met with the elders and told then of Pharaohs new command.

"I have angered the Pharaoh and he has commanded that the slaves must now gather their own reeds and straw to make the bricks and still meet the required number of bricks every day." Moses sadly announced,

The elders were angry, some cried, and they pointed at Moses and blamed him for this extra hardship they would have to endure.

I growled at them for their lack of trust and faith.

Moses was very troubled and prayed.

God answered and said, "The Pharaoh will soon see and feel the powers of God and he will comply."

The following day we again entered the palace and approached Pharaoh.

"You have returned," he said angrily. "Do you desire that I inflict greater work demands upon my slaves?"

Moses handed his staff to Aaron and as God had instructed he dropped it to the floor and it became a snake. It hissed and squirmed on the floor and started to crawl towards Pharaoh.

Pharaoh did not fail to recognize just as he used his priests and assistants to carry out his commands Moses used Aaron. Thus Pharaoh began to consider Moses as a leader and perhaps even royalty.

He quickly instructed his seven priests to drop their staffs and they also became snakes, hissing and crawling about.

I never liked snakes. They always had tried to eat a baby goat or sheep but I had learned how to protect my flocks and defeat any snake. The snake from Moses's staff began to attack the other seven snakes. With my ferocious bark I quickly jumped in and bit one, right behind its vile head, clamping down as hard as I could. The snake was done. Moses's snake was swallowing one and I whirled and bit on down on the head of another and finished that one off too. Before you could say One Pharaoh, Two Pharaohs, Three Pharaohs, between me and the good snake we had knocked off all seven of the others.

Aaron was shaking a bit, he was so surprised and frightened about what had just happened but he remembered and quickly grabbed Moses's snake by the tail and it became a staff again. It was quite a bit wider and fatter than it had been, I guess because of the snakes it had swallowed. I think if it had stayed a snake it would have had quite a stomach ache.

The Pharaoh's priests were very upset about what had just occurred. They knew they were in trouble, or in the doghouse as some people would say, but I don't know why because I like dog houses.

Pharaoh looked at them in a very angry way and dismissed them, calling them incompetent.

I heard one of them whisper to another "I needed my staff to help me walk. What am I going to use now?"

"Help you walk?" Pharaoh thundered. "Your weak magic has embarrassed us. I should have your legs cut off so you would crawl like a snake! Be gone before I utter that command."

The priests quickly scuttled away.

"This proves nothing Moses. The Israelites will remain as my slaves. Now go!"

We left again and again we were sad. Moses again prayed and God spoke to him, instructing him to bring his staff and wait the next morning at Pharaoh's favorite spot by the Nile.

We did so the next morning. Aaron told us that the Egyptian people had a strong reverence for the Nile as it was this river's water that supported their way of life. The water was used to drink, bath, water their crops and livestock or dip in to cool off. The fish they caught from the Nile River provided an important part of their food.

Now Pharaoh would come to the river every morning to check the water level and to express gratitude to their God of the Nile.

That morning we waited as Pharaoh came to the water's edge. This was his favorite spot. The current of the Nile had rounded out a small lagoon of the river where the water flowed gently, circling in small eddies. The water here was clear and free of crocodiles. Palm trees lined the banks. White egrets waded along the shallows, then quickly plunged their head into the water coming up with a fish in their beak. An eagle circled high above, floating on the updrafts. The air was hot and had a moist aroma.

It was this spot that years ago the Pharaohs' daughter had discovered a floating basket and on investigating had found a baby boy in the basket.

That baby had been Moses, so named as the name meant, drawn from the river. That Pharaoh those years ago was Seti I, the father of Ramses II, the current Pharaoh.

Ramses II approached with his two guards and a servant who was fanning him with a large fan made of Peacock feathers. He was agitated as he saw Moses, Aaron and of course, me, awaiting him. "Beware Moses! You are exhausting my patience. I have had enough of you."

"It is not I that makes this demand of you, it is God, the one supreme God. God has sent me to say, let my people go, but you have refused so now you shall see the power of God and be fearful."

I barked, telling Moses for a person that had trouble speaking he sure was eloquent.

Moses gave me a look to be still. He had Aaron lift Moses's staff and Aaron struck the water of the Nile.

The water began to turn red, as red as the color of blood.

Pharaoh was shocked. He fell to his knees and prayed to Hapi, the Egyptian God of the Nile to restore the water to its clear color but it remained red.

The Egyptians were very superstitious and thought the water had actually turned to blood. I sniffed and realized it was the same problem we had at a pond back home. I had been guarding the goats and sheep on a very warm, humid day, and the pond had turned red. It was filled with red algae. My parents explained that algae were plants without roots. They were always around the water but sometimes, when conditions were ripe, they would rapidly multiply and fill a body of water, such as a pond, a lake, and in rare instances, now the Nile. The red algae bloom covered the water and the plants quickly absorbed all the oxygen in the water. The fish in the Nile could not live without oxygen and they died their bodies floating on the surface. The polluted red water and the dead fish gave off a very stinky odor. Of course nothing could drink from or use any of this water now. I heard the Egyptians whispering, "The God of the Israelites turned the Nile water into blood." They were terrified.

Pharaoh ordered the slaves to dig wells in order to tap into underground water sources at the palace and at some of the main crossroads of the city. Those that were wealthy also had their slaves dig wells.

Thus Pharaoh, his family and close associates, the wealthy and some others had drinking water and were not so terribly effected. The majority of the people had no water now which in the very hot climate was a serious catastrophe.

The Israelites, the men, who had dug these wells were exhausted and not able to dig their own wells as they returned to their village. Moses however gave specific directions to Miriam describing the location of the oasis where Aaron had waited for him. The water there was clear and fresh. Miriam had the women go to that oasis and they brought many water bags to fill. They struggled to bring these now-heavy bags back to their home but succeeded, and the Israelites made do with these bags of life- saving water.

After seven days had passed God instructed Moses to return to the Pharaoh. Pharaoh still refused to let the Israelites go free. Moses warned that a plague of frogs would follow. Did it?

CHAPTER 7

I realized what God had done. The water of the Nile, overflowing with red algae, depleted of oxygen, polluted with dead fish, and a terrible smelly odor could not sustain any life. The frogs, unable to remain in or near the Nile were desperately seeking other sources of water. The wells that were dug, containing fresh water, drew the frogs as magnets draw metal. The frogs were almost everywhere trying to find water. As there were no wells in the Israelites village the frogs did not go there, but on the palace grounds the place was soon overrun with frogs. Big frogs, little frogs, green frogs, spotted frogs, even red frogs. Pharaoh, as well as all his people, discovered it was grossly unpleasant to hear a pop and feel a squish under your sandals when you accidently stepped on a frog. Sitting on one was even worse. Sometimes you started to get ready to eat your dinner and realized your dinner was looking back at you because it wasn't dinner, it was a big, green, hopping, bulgy-eyed frog saying. "Grumph."

Pharaoh sent a messenger to Moses to return. He did and Pharaoh asked Moses to have God remove the frogs and he would allow the Israelites to go to the mountain and sacrifice to their God.

Moses was happy to do so.

About this time the red algae died off, the water was flowing and clear again, the frogs that were still alive, happily hopped back to the Nile and the fish returned. The Egyptians swept up the many, many frogs that had been squashed and piled them in heaps. The odor was very bad so people used scarves to cover their nostrils.

When Pharaoh saw the Nile was flowing and the frogs were gone he had a change of heart.

"I have changed my mind. The Israelites may not go free!"

We were very angry that he had lied. I did my liar, liar dance;

"Liar, liar you'll be sad, 'cause when you lie things will be bad."

Aaron now took Moses's staff, as God had instructed Moses, and struck the earth. Crawly, itch- causing insects now appeared everywhere. They were lice, fleas, sandflies, mosquitoes and gnats and they arose throughout all the land of Egypt.

Aaron again struck the earth and now an army of mice and rats descended upon the people of Egypt.

Pharaoh commanded his priests to cast magic spells to make all these things be gone but the priests begged to be forgiven stating, "Their God's power is greater oh Pharaoh. Now Pharaoh realized he was dealing with a force mightier than his.

I think I understood the natural progression of what God had brought about. The red algae took the oxygen out of the Nile causing the fish to die and the frogs to leave. The dead fish, dead frogs and inability of the people to bathe and keep clean, attracted the bugs and vermin that followed.

I was very worried about the rise in fleas but, whew, they stayed away from the Israelites village. We had not dug any wells so did not draw in the frogs and as we did not have dead frogs the insects and vermin were not drawn to our area. The water the women kept bringing from the oasis was sufficient for drinking and washing.

The next day Pharaoh was still angry and stubborn and again said, "No, the Israelites will not be free."

Now God caused a swarm of locusts, so many that the sky grew dark as they came flying in.

Locusts which landed on the crops and devoured them until the fields which had been thick with wheat and other grains were now barren and dead. Where there had been green stems abundant with seeds, there were now decaying brown bits of dead plants. The fields had been ravaged.

Pharaoh knew in his heart he was defeated but he was stubborn and his mind refused to accept it. Again Pharaoh told Moses he would release the slaves and Moses prayed to God to remove the swarms of insects The insects left but again Pharaoh told Moses he still would not let the Israelites go.

The poor hygiene caused by lack of water and the piles of dead frogs and fish had brought swarms of vermin, insects that bit the cattle and sheep as well as people causing diseases. The Egyptian people were suffering.

Their cattle were dying. The people were ill with diseases and infections from the bites of various insects. A delegation of the Egyptian elders along with Pharaoh's advisors came to meet with him and plead with him to release the Israelites from slavery. He refused.

Moses was troubled. He had faith and had followed Gods instructions but Pharaoh still would not free the people from slavery.

Moses sat with his family around him, his sister Miriam, his mother, Jochabed, and Aaron and his wife and sons.

"God told me he would harden Pharaoh's heart and it is so, but our people are suffering even more because of me." Moses said.

Miriam and Aaron were downcast and even Jochabed was sad. A date tree, a type of palm tree, grew by the courtyard. I had to do something. I barked and when I had their attention I ran to the tree and jumped up to try to grab a fruit from the tree, a date. It was high and not easy for me to reach. Moses and the others were watching me. Miriam laughed, she thought this was funny. I jumped again and again, higher and higher. No date. Finally I gathered my strength and jumped as high as I could and I got it. I got the date. I brought it over to Moses, wagging my tail. This was an especially good date because I had worked so hard to get it. I saw Moses face light up. He understood.

"Yes!" he said. "If it were easy people would not appreciate it. It's because if it is so hard to accomplish and then people cherish it. So it is with God. The people would not value it if came too easily. That's why God hardened Pharaoh's heart and now I know that it is Gods' plan that our people shall be free."

The others understood it as Moses stated and nodded their heads in agreement.

I had saved the day, again, but did they recognize it?

Moses winked at me. He did.

The children still thought it was so funny to see me jumping and did not connect the message. However Aaron and the other adults understood.

But Moses was troubled and worried about his wife, Zipporah and their two sons. He wanted them to be safe, away from this turmoil. They were not slaves and were free to leave. It tore at his heart to part with them but he sent them with two men to protect them back to Midian and Jethro, Zipporah's father.

CHAPTER 8

God instructed Moses to have the Israelites move their animals indoors for a hail storm of huge icy balls of hail would soon deluge upon the land and it was so. With thunder and lightning large ice balls of hail along with ice so cold that it burst into flames showered upon Egypt.

Trees were shattered and people or animals struck by this hail were badly injured.

Still Pharaoh was unyielding. He had prayed to Hapi, God of the Nile, but that had failed to restore the natural waters of the Nile after the river had turned red and now he prayed to all the Gods of Egypt but his prayers were of no avail.

The sun God, Ra, was one of the strongest, mightiest Egyptian Gods, and now Pharaoh watched in disbelief as the sun grew dimmer and the day was covered with the darkness of the darkest nights.

Deserted by his Gods, rejected by his people, Pharaoh grew in despair but resolved that he would not release the Israelites.

Now I admit. I was scared. I never saw hail and fire like that. Oh, I had seen thunderstorms and hail but never the hailstones the size of these. And this darkness. Not natural.

Moses saw me trying to crawl under the blankets.

"Don't fear, God will protect."

"I don't like this darkness. I can't see if there is danger around and I'm a guardian dog."

"When I was in school in the palace, as a child, I was taught by those who had studied the sky." Moses told me. "The darkness is caused by an eclipse. The Moon is between us and the sun and is blocking the golden bright rays of the sun. It will pass and the bright daylight will be back."

"Doesn't Pharaoh know this?" I wondered.

"He does but that this came about as God commanded and his Gods were powerless to prevent it. This has left him feeling impotent. He is defeated."

Yet God had another plague to bring upon Pharaoh. A plague that was created by Seti I, the father of Pharaoh when he ordered the Hebrew male babies to be killed. As that Pharaoh commanded now so shall it be for the Egyptian people.

Moses felt Gods intentions and pleaded with God to avert this decree.

"It has been brought upon them by their own words. You are to instruct the Israelites to take a lambs blood and smear it upon their door that they shall be spared tonight, but in all homes not so marked the first born male in that home shall surely perish tonight."

Moses quickly sent messengers throughout Goshen so the Israelites were able to protect their households. Some who had been treated kindly by the Egyptians, brought them into their homes also, to provide protection and those Egyptians were safe. Others throughout the land saw their fathers or brothers, or sons, those who were first-born, perish.

In the morning cries of anguish were heard and Pharaoh sent a messenger to Moses.

The message was, "Take your people, your flocks, your possessions and leave Egypt at once."

The news spread quickly. People cheered and screamed with joy. The donkeys brayed, the goats bleated, cows mooed, dogs were barking and children laughing. People quickly packed their little belongings that they could carry. Some were fortunate to have carts that their donkeys pulled.

Some Egyptian people did not blame the Israelites for the disasters brought by the plagues. They felt guilty that they had treated the Israelites badly and gave them food, bags of water, gold, jewels and livestock to take with them. The same livestock, sheep, goats, donkeys, and cattle that as slaves, the Israelites, had tended for their owners.

One Egyptian remembered that it was the ancestor of the Israelites, Joseph, who had led Egypt through a seven year period of draught and famine. His planning had provided the food and water needed during that terrible time, and the Egyptians had been very grateful to Joseph.

Some gave them weapons so they would have some protection in the dangerous wilderness they were heading into. The weapons were mostly not in good condition. The bows needed bow-strings, the swords were dull and rusty and the metal spearheads were loose on their poles and needed to be tied on securely.

So it began. Their journey as they started to depart from Egypt in a mass migration.

CHAPTER 9

They left in haste. What if Pharaoh again changed his mind? They took the bread that was baking in their ovens that had no time to rise. They called that flat bread matzah.

I thought, "I bet they'll have a holiday every year to remember leaving Egypt. They'll celebrate that death passed over their homes and they'll eat matzah instead of regular bread for the remembrance. Maybe they'll call it, Flat bread day?",

One man, Nachson ben Amanidav, loudly voiced his complaints to Moses.

"Where shall we go? What shall we eat? How shall we survive?"

"Would you rather remain a slave, you and your children?" Moses rebuked him.

"No, I would not, but marching straight into this unforgiving desert causes me great concerns. Are we to escape slavery but perish in the desert?" Nachson asked.

"God shall provide." Moses replied.

There was no order to this march. It was chaotic. People were loudly calling to one another, as families were becoming separated, babies were crying and small children were getting lost. Groups of people, some carrying babies, some pushing carts, some fortunate enough to have a donkey pulling their cart, many carrying the few possessions they had, created a jostling, near-gridlock entanglement. Some groups headed to the right and others to the left. Angry voices were raised as collisions occurred. Dust rose about our eyes and nostrils as the sand swirled around.

Some tended flocks of sheep and goats. The donkeys and some of the other animals bumped into the crowds of people, knocking over the small children who were in danger of being trampled.

With my sense of keeping order, from my days as herding the flocks, the chaos was agonizing.

I barked loudly to Moses, he heard and stopped the procession. He also had shepherded the flocks and had this same sense of bringing order and control. Moses called for the elders of each of the twelve tribes to meet with him.

The heads of the twelve tribes sat down with Moses. These were the sons of Jacob. Reuben, Simeon, Levi, Judah, Issachar, Zebulon, Benjamin, Dan, Naphtali, Gad, Asher and Joseph. Moses instructed that the people would march in order behind the heads of their tribe The tribe that grew from the eldest son shall be the first and the second born the next, and so on. Those people fleeing from Egypt who are not Israelites shall form behind the last tribe. In the rear shall be all the flocks and spare animals. Each tribe shall select thirty young men who shall be our guardians. Each group of thirty shall appoint a captain. The captains shall send two men to scout at a distance in front of us, two to patrol along the distant hills to our sides, and two to take up our rear. The guardians were armed with weapons taken from Egypt, bows and arrows, swords and spears. It would be a while before they learned how to use these effectively. Thus did Moses bring order were there was chaos.

The elders returned to their tribes, now organized along the structure set up by Moses, and we proceeded.

And God set before them a column of clouds during the day, and a column of fire at night to mark the path.

Nachson still worried. "I see so many problems ahead." He called to Moses. "Are we doing the right thing?"

"Have faith in God." Moses replied.

What lay ahead?

CHAPTER 10

The danger came not from ahead but from behind.

Many of the Egyptians were now angry at Pharaoh for releasing the slaves. Couriers were sent to Pharaoh expressing their displeasure. He became very angry and disturbed at himself for releasing the slaves. He called to his generals to have their warriors mount their chariots and swiftly pursue the Israelites and destroy them.

"You are using fast horses and they are on foot. It should be no challenge to overtake and run them down!" he ordered.

Six hundred of his fastest chariots and all the other war chariots in Egypt now rode after the Israelites.

Along with the driver were one or two warriors, expert with bows, spears and swords. There were six hundred thousand men, plus women and children among the Israelites, but none had the training of these proven warriors. Even if they had the skills it was hopeless to stand on foot against a charge of war chariots. The Israelites had come to the Sea of Reeds.

Now I was an excellent swimmer using, of course, the dog paddle. But Moses knew the slaves had never earned their swimmers certificates. They did not have the luxury of swimming pools nor did they have the time to learn to swim in the river. They had been busy working in the fields and building the Pharaoh's cities. They just could not swim.

The scouts from the rear had seen the clouds of dusty sand made by hundreds of galloping horses pulling the chariots. They saw far in the distance the attacking army of Egyptians heading towards them.

They quickly sent messages to Moses of the disaster that was approaching.

The people heard the frightening news and were terrified.

"Told you there would be problems." Nachson called out.

"Moses, have you brought us here to perish by the Egyptian chariots? We have no defense against them." They cried out to Moses and to their God.

God directed Moses to lift his staff and hold it over the sea and Moses, with faith in his God, did as Instructed. The water was still high.

Moses cried out to all. "God will cause the waters to part but first we must show our faith. I need at least one person to move into the waters. Have no fear for God will protect you."

No one responded.

"Show your faith in God!" Moses called out. No one moved.

They could not swim and feared they would drown.

One man, named Nachson ben Amanidav, spoke. "Moses, did you think we had a club house with a swimming pool, that we got our swimming merit badge, or that we had time to bathe in the Nile? We slaved seven days a week and the only water that fell upon my body was when I had time to splash some water from a bowl, apply a washcloth, and clean up a bit."

"One must do this or we shall all perish." Moses replied.

Nachson looked around. No one moved. They all were looking at him. "Okay." He muttered.

He slowly stepped into the water. He stopped as the cool water lapped around his toes. He took a deep breath and moved forward until the water was up to his knees. He looked at Moses and Moses nodded and encouraged him to move forward. Nachson took a gulp of air and moved until the water was up his belly. He stopped and froze in place. He may have moved forward again but he may not have. The waters would not part until he moved forward and the Egyptians grew closer.. I decided to act. I jumped in and pushed his back with my nose. That little push was all he needed to get his legs moving forward again. The water was up to his nostrils. Suddenly there was a shaking, violent trembling of the ground and people grabbed anything for support. Some fell over but when the earth stopped moving under their feet they stood again. The base under the sea had pushed up to form a land bridge stretching from the bank of the river, where the Israelites stood, to the opposite shore. The man, Nachson, now stood on the ground. It was muddy but he was able to move forward and went as fast as he could towards the opposite shore. The people saw the way was clear and they followed, keeping the marching order, following their tribal elders.

But there were thousands and it would take hours for all to cross.

God now moved a column of clouds between the approaching Egyptian chariots and the people.

What was this cloud? Fog? A thick cloud of sand dust and smoke from the shaking of the Earth? A fissure deep into the earth, releasing sulfuric smoke?

The Egyptians had to stop. The cloud blinded them. They could not see what was in front of them nor could their panicked horses who refused to move forward in this thick cloud.

The Israelites rushed onto the land bridge, moving and running, to get to the opposite shore.

Now the last tribe had crossed and the others that had fled Egypt, slaves from different nations crossed over and now the flocks of sheep, goats and cattle, driven by shepherds and me.

Moses and I were the last to cross.

We were on the opposite bank of the Red Sea but how long would the cloud hold back the Egyptians?

Now the cloud was breaking up and we could see the chariots forming up again. What was to stop them from pursuing us over the land bridge and attack us?

The Egyptian chariots, archers, swordsmen and horsemen now were galloping and thundering across the land bridge and were almost upon us.

Moses looked to God who told him to raise his rod over the waters. The first horses of the Egyptians were starting up the river bank. My fur on my neck stood upright as I saw this. Moses raised his staff and the earth again shook violently and abruptly the waters rushed back again, as a huge wave, knocking into the sea the horses that had started up the bank. The waters closed over the Egyptians.

With their heavy armor the men could not swim. The chariots sunk to the bottom of the sea as did the drivers and the archers, swordsmen and horsemen. As the water grew calmer we saw, further downstream, many of the horses managed to swim to shore safely.

It was a miracle that the Egyptians had not reached us and we now were surely free. There was no doubt that God had provided.

Moses raised his arms in joyful prayer to God, singing of God's greatness and the men joined him in song praising the wonders of God. The women shrilled a high chanting triumphant sound. Then Miriam took her timbral and led the women in a triumphant song and dance for they had not only survived the unimaginable but had witnessed a miracle.

"We do not sing over the sad death of the Egyptian warriors for all life is holy but we sing for our freedom and we praise God who has seen over us and provided for us."

I barked and barked in joy circling my tail in a frenzy, released from the fear that we would all have perished.

The men slaughtered many lambs, following Gods instructions for cooking and which parts were permitted for eating and which would be set aside as their sacrifice to the almighty.

The dancing, feasting and prayers of gratitude went on through the night.

Aaron took Moses aside. Aaron was wise and had seen much of human nature.

"I fear that generations to come will not believe what we have witnessed with our own eyes." He stated over the noises of celebration. "We must tell and retell our children and make it their duty to tell their children, so these amazing events shall be known as their heritage."

Moses simply replied, "And so it will be."

Moses saw Nachson, the brave man who had waded into the Sea.

"You were very courageous, yet I thought you of all would be the last person to volunteer." Moses told him. "I thought you were afraid."

"I am concerned when I see problems but if the solution is for me to act, then I act. Don't compare concern about problems with cowardice." Nachson replied.

"You are correct and I apologize." Moses responded.

I was glad he did for it takes a big man to admit he has been wrong. I also gave Moses an encouraging "woof".

As for Pharaoh. The news reached him that his army had perished and the Israelites were forever beyond his reach. He reacted with a temper tantrum, gnashing his teeth, ordering the death of the person who brought the news, smashing vases that were by his side and commanding that the name of Moses and all records of the Israelites be stricken, removed, wiped off all documents and places. There shall be no history, no mention in Egypt that this ever occurred and never shall the name Moses be uttered for the person doing so shall be put to death.

CHAPTER 11

They rested, then Moses roused them to begin their long march. They were now free, no longer fearful that Egyptian warriors were pursuing them. They formed into the tribes following their elders in the marching order Moses had prescribed. Three days they walked without food nor water. The hot desert sun took their strength but still they walked. They grumbled about the lack of water and knew they would not survive if they failed to find water.

God heard their cries and spoke to Moses.

"Have I not proven that I shall provide? Why do they doubt and complain?"

Moses had no answer. They are just mortals God. They are imperfect."

God told Moses, "Let Polaris locate your water for I have given him a strong sense of smell."

I sniffed and sure enough I caught a whiff of water in the distance. I swerved and ran towards it. We came upon a body of water but the water was bitter to the taste and they could not drink. Moses tossed a piece of wood, that God showed him, into the water and the water was now sweet and the people drank of the water and provided for their animals.

They had good water now but they had run out of food.

Again they complained, "What are we to eat? We could slaughter more lambs."

"No!" Moses replied. "God will lead us to our own land but there men will judge our wealth by the size of our flocks. We shall not appear as paupers. If we start slaughtering the herds for food they shall quickly be gone. No, we must see to it that the herds flourish and multiply. God will see to our needs."

"Still they complain." Said God.

"They are hungry." Moses replied. "They are good people, they have faith, and they have seen the wondrous acts you have performed."

God caused the desert plants to bloom covering the desert with white blossoms and berries.

God instructed the Israelites that they should gather the berries for food but only enough for one day but on the sixth day, Friday, they should gather a double portion for they were to rest on the Sabbath and refrain from any labor.

The food was prepared properly and was creamy and rich tasting in their mouths.

Some gathered more than one days' portion to only discover that overnight the food, which was called "manna", had spoiled and was now rotten to the taste. Some of them then fell ill.

"You were foolish and greedy", the other people told them. "God said only one days' portion. You should have obeyed."

The desert plants also provided the sustenance for the flocks of sheep, goats, donkeys and cattle.

Every day they would gather the Manna, form their marching order and trudge on.

Again the thirsty need for water arose. Moses sent me to scout ahead for water.

After a while I picked up the scent. It was strong. I waited until Moses and the people caught up to me then we came to a place of abundant water. Here they rested, refreshed themselves, watered the sheep, goats, cattle and donkeys and filled their water bags. It was now the Sabbath and we spent the day in relaxation, lying back on the grass surrounding the bodies of water, enjoying the clouds overhead and at night watching God's display of the thousands of brilliant stars in the sky and the occasional shooting star causing the children to murmur in glee and awe.

Moses whispered to me, "This is better than watching television."

That drew a blank for me. What is television?

"Oops." He said. "Something I saw in the future but I forgot you wouldn't know about it."

Aaron spoke to Moses about the people.

"They were born as slaves and have known only slavery. Yes, now we are free, but they still think as slaves. When you are a slave, as we were in Egypt, you think only of today. You work under the hot sun and hope you will be spared the lash and perhaps you will be rewarded with some extra rations of food and water. You do not think of the future for you and your children have no future, you only think of how to get through each day, one at a time. They learned to plea for food and water for the day. So now, they whine and cry when they are thirsty or hungry because they cannot even hope that the water will be there tomorrow. They are unable to think about tomorrows. It will take time for them to learn. Be patient with them."

And Moses understood.

We had developed a routine. Every morning the children would go out to gather the manna and when they returned the women would prepare it. The shepherds would water the goats, sheep, donkeys and cattle. The three hundred and sixty young men who served as scouts and guardians would send out a few as lookouts while the others practiced their archery with bow and arrow and the use of swords and spears.   The twelve captains of these men, one from each of the twelve tribes, had elected one to be their leader. He was Joshua, the son of Nun. Joshua our Commander they called him. Joshua had instructed the captains and the others to select and train the other men so they would also become skilled with these weapons, and every evening, when they made camp, the men would take time to practice.

Moses saw this and it was good.

CHAPTER 12

We continued on our march and were now nearing Mount Horeb. Water again was scarce and the people and animals were again very thirsty, dangerously thirsty, for in the heat of the desert water equals survival. I sniffed for the aroma of water but my sniffer found nothing. I felt I had failed and held my tail between my legs. Moses reassured me that God was watching over us and would provide. And God did. God directed Moses to a large rock on the side of a hill and told Moses to raise his staff and strike the rock. Now this I had to see. There was absolutely no hint of water by that rock and I wondered what would happen? Would Moses striking the rock cause lightening to appear and a thunderstorm? Would the rock roll away and reveal an entrance to a cave with a long tunnel leading to an underground lake? No, it wasn't that at all. Moses struck the rock and it split in two and water started to gush out. Real water, cool and clear. The water flowed down the hill and formed a huge pool at the base. The people drank and the water tasted good and was refreshing and cleansing. They again filled their water-skins then let the animals drink to their fill. Afterwards the people bathed in the water.

Now Moses father-in-law, Jethro, had heard that Moses and the Israelites were making camp within a two days journey and he came to visit, bringing Moses' wife, Zipporah and their two sons.

Jethro had been anxious to visit Moses and reunite him with his wife and grandchildren.

"It is good for a family to spend time together." he told Moses.

Moses wanted to spend more time with Jethro but every evening he would hold court, listening to the grievances and complaints of the people. There were many. There were complaints about misuse or improper taking of possessions, of mistreatment of as family member by another, of husbands and wives quarrels, and a myriad of assorted problems. Moses would hear all sides, consider the issues and render a judgement. The hearings went on late into every night.

Jethro was a wise man and spoke to Moses. "You should not do this by yourself. It is too much.

You should select honest, righteous, devout men from each tribe, and they should sit as judges and hear these disputes. Not you alone."

Moses listened and he respected Jethro's voice and he agreed.

I barked my agreement too.

"I will do as you suggest for it is a good plan. I know the heat of the desert and the stress our people are feeling leads to quick tempers and petty disputes. They are basically good people however."

Moses did then select judges as Jethro had suggested.

After some time Jethro had to depart and return to his home. Before doing so he learned of all the miracles God had brought for the Israelites and he acknowledged that their God was the one and supreme God. We were sad when he left but he said he would visit again. He promised to give my love to Felicia and the pups and tell them I missed them.

We again proceeded on our march. The elderly had a difficult time keeping up and Moses had directed that they go to the rear, just in front of the herds. The animals took their time anyway, and they would catch up to the rest of in the evening. Others who became ill or injured also went to the rear and were placed in some of the animal-drawn carts. The desert floor, shifting sands and many small rocks to catch and twist the legs of the unwary, also caused many injuries. Some with twisted ankles stayed with their tribe while others rode on the carts in the rear. The desert was also very hard on the animals and some perished. Those who did were not suitable for sacrifice to God, and we used every part of the animal, nothing would be wasted. The good meat would be cooked in the evening or sliced and dried on racks in the hot sun for snacks. The skin would be prepared also. Thin strips of skin were used for bow-strings and to tie and reinforce the steel points of the spears. The strips also repaired the harnesses and were useful as ropes. Some of the soft sheepskins were used to wrap the newborn babies, as many of the woman were giving birth along our way.

Some of the woman were also placed in the carts at the rear, with their babies, following childbirth.

I saw something different in the young children who had been born in the desert on our journey.

They were growing up in the desert and did not seem to suffer in the heat and could go for longer distances without water. They seemed tougher and prouder than the ones who had grown up as slaves.

They tended to stand their ground and were ready to fight to defend their turf. These were traits that would be needed.

CHAPTER 13

We were passing through lands occupied by other people. Some offered hospitality. Some did not.

We journeyed on in our usual formation. The scouts did not report any concerns. Then from the rear, where travelled the elderly, ill, women and babies we heard screams. We were under attack but the attack came not from the front where our men were, but from the rear where they were helpless.

It was the way of cowards. They had waited until the scouts passed then snuck down from the hills on both sides, let loose a swarm of arrows, then attacked with swords, spears and axes. Moses quickly called Joshua to bring his men to defend the rear. I went running with Joshua and his warriors. We were furious. We got to the rear where the enemy had slaughtered those that could not defend themselves. Now they would face men and dog. We were not battle hardened but we were ready. Our enemy were the cowardly, Amalek and the Amalekites.

Moses climbed to the top of the hill with Aaron and the son of Miriam, Hur. Moses lifted his arms holding his staff over his head. Joshua and the men were struggling but the sight of Moses with his staff gave them renewed energy and they began to deflect the swords of the Amalekites and then strike with their own sword. The enemy began falling and they started to retreat. Moses however tired and his arms could not stay up. Now the enemy reformed and started to overcome our men. I was in the midst of it, biting a leg then pulling the enemy warrior on the ground where a spear thrust by one of our guys put an end to him. No more help-less women would he kill.

Aaron and Hur helped Moses again raise his arms and again we surged forward, first a volley of arrows from our bows, many finding their mark, then we ran to them with our spears at waist high plunging into their bod-ies, followed by our swords slashing and disposing of them. When Moses's arms fell we found ourselves being beaten but when he again raised the staff we would rush them again, pushing them back and back until finally they broke and ran from us.

They were defeated.

We suffered casualties also and the loss of many good men. The camp was in mourning for the entire week. Life had to go on. We had to go on. We tended to the injuries of the wounded.

I had a bandage on my right front paw where it had been cut by a spear that had just missed inflicting serious damage. I was lucky but I was mov-ing so fast it was hard for them to hit me.

Joshua replaced those who had died with new men. Some of the young women also insisted that they could fight and they became skilled archers. It was unheard of for women to be warriors but they insisted and the men agreed. It was good, for in days to come later, the women proved how valu-able their archery was. We became more cautious as we proceeded.

We arrived in the Sinai wilderness and something wonderful was go-ing to happen.

CHAPTER 14

We made camp by Mount Sinai. God's mountain. It was high though not the highest mountain. We found a good source of water and we had ample food with manna. People though had grown weary with the same diet of manna and God had provided thousands of gulls that we caught, prepared and enjoyed until we were stuffed. Some of the people had eaten so much they actually got terribly bad stomach aches and never wanted to taste gull again.. One should not be a glutton.

Moses and I climbed up the mountain and God was there. God spoke to Moses as I listened.

"I have brought you from slavery to freedom. Now if the descendants of Abraham shall keep my covenant I shall make you a holy people, a priestly people, a light to the nations."

We climbed back down the mountain and Moses gathered all the people. The elders of each tribe stood by his side, as did Aaron. After hearing what God had proposed the people, almost in unison, eagerly agreed to abide by God's laws and the covenant.

One elderly wise man questioned. "Would God allow something horrendous to happen to us as an example to the nations? Something so terrible that all mankind would say, this must never happen to any people again? Is that what a light to the nations might mean?"

The others did not consider this thought.

We climbed back up the mountain and Moses reported that the people had accepted.

Wow, I was tired from climbing up and down and up and down.

God told Moses it was good and now the people must prepare for the third day, for on that day God shall come down the mountain and appear to the people in a cloud of smoke. The people shall purify themselves in advance of the third day. They shall bathe, wash their clothing and men and women shall not embrace. No one shall approach the mountain until I instruct them, for to do so would mean death.

When the ram's horn is heard they may then approach.

And the people did as instructed.

We were trembling with anticipation. I was so excited I could not sleep at night and stood in the darkness just staring at the mountain.

On the third day, early in the morning, we arose to find the earth trembling. The mountain was shaking, covered in smoke and flames could be seen at the top. The people were so enthusiastic they were shaking also.

We heard the louds blast of the ram's horn and Moses led us from the camp to the base of Mount Sinai and the people stood in awe.

God spoke and his words were as thunder and he called Moses to climb the mountain and Moses and I did so.

Moses held on to my collar as we climbed and I helped pull him up.

Should I have gone up with Moses? We were inseparable, together as one and God seemed to have no objection.

God had Moses also bring Aaron up the mountain.

God spoke giving them his laws we were to follow and we descended.

Moses was to return with seventy of the elders, along with Aaron and Hur, with Joshua assisting, and we did return to the mountain where God appeared. All witnessed this. The people, other than the seventy selected, remained below. God commanded then that Moses alone climb to the top where Moses was to carve onto two tablets the words of God. If anyone else approached God would smite them.

Joshua, the seventy tribal leaders, and me, waited part way up the mountain for Moses return.

Aaron went back to the main camp with the people. We made our camp there, on the mountain, and waited.

What were these laws, these commandments? Ten were written upon the two tablets but six hundred and three additional were spoken by word alone.

I later learned these commands were summarized in four areas.

I am the one, supreme God. You shall have no others. You shall never worship idols, statues, or images. The temple alone, that you shall build, shall be your holy site. You shall not use the name of the Lord, or pray, for trivial, unimportant matters such as gambling or that you might score while playing baseball or other sports.

The people looked quizzically at one another with that one and were heard to ask, "What's baseball?"

"That will come years from now." Moses replied.

You shall be caring of one another, honest in your dealings, shall not take another's belongings nor shall you kill another. I have seen that when a man dies his widow and children are made to provide for themselves or are sold into slavery. This shall not be! You are to provide for the widow, the orphan, the ill and infirmed and those unable to care for themselves. As Jethro provided hospitality to Moses you are to provide hospitality for all in need. If one injures another you may return an equal but not excessive injury, or arrange reasonable compensation.

I have provided a world with trees for shade and lumber for building, abundant fish in the seas that you may harvest, animals in the fields that you may utilize for work and for a source of food and birds of the air or on the ground whose eggs you may take. I have given you a wonderful place but you shall be the care-takers and build a better world. You make take a tree for your use but you must plant a seedling to replace it. You may use animals for work or food but you may not abuse them.

You are to treat animals in a humane manner. I have seen men slay a calf and boil it in its mother's milk. Such practice is callous and horrendous to me and shall cease. You may take what you need only. If you are to slaughter an animal for food it must be disposed of with one swift cut.

Animals were not created for your sport. Unclean animals, such as pigs that wallow in garbage, scavengers, shellfish and predators, are forbidden for your food, now and forever and ever.

You may fish for your needs but if you overfish surely the fish will disappear.

You may harvest the eggs of birds but you must first shoo away the parents so they shall not see you harvest their eggs.

You are to build a temple for God according to God's description and shall observe the holidays that God has set. The tablets carved by Moses shall be carried in an ark according to God's description.

The seventh day of each week, Saturday, the Sabbath, is a day to refrain from work and rest. It is a day devoted to thoughts, family and joy.

Those words summarized to me the commandments of the creator, of God.

I thought about them a lot. They did provide a wonderful blueprint for a good life for everyone.

CHAPTER 15

Moses spent 40 days and forty nights atop the mountain. We waited part way up where we had made camp under the shade of some trees, near a pond. We were getting very worried about Moses. After one week had passed Joshua sent me to go up to the top, to Moses, bringing bags of food and water, strapped to my sides. I was very scared as I climbed up. Would God allow me to approach or would he smite me? After a climb I approached, crawling forward. Moses saw me. I hesitated. Moses smiled and beckoned me to approach. He told me that God was laughing and said your Polaris is a very brave and loyal dog. Moses was glad to get the supplies. Very relieved that I was not smitten and relieved that Moses was alive and well I returned to our base camp. My tail was wagging when I arrived back and saw Joshua and the others and my happy bark let them know that all was good.

Joshua sent me back up once a week. Once I found Moses so deep in concentration that he was unaware of me. There was a glow about him. I slipped off the packs of food and water and left.

We at the base camp, Joshua and the seventy tribal elders, knew Moses was communicating with God and all was well. The people below however had no communication from us and must have been very concerned about Moses and all of us. We should have sent word to them but we did not.

After forty days and nights Moses came down. He was carrying two stone tablets with the words of God etched upon them. His face shone with and his step was invigorated. He momentarily stopped, said nothing, and waited as we quickly broke camp and proceeded down the mountain with him. Joshua and I were at his side.

We approached the main camp of the people and what we saw was astounding and terrible.

After all God had done for these people I could not believe what they now had done.

They were dancing, singing, circling and worshipping a golden calf.

Moses was so furious, and you know Moses has always had a problem with his temper.

He took the two holy tablets and threw them to the ground, causing them to shatter.

The people looked down as they were ashamed to look Moses in the eye.

"After all you have witnessed God as done you this is how you respond?" he yelled.

Some of the people now became angry at Moses. I growled at them and they stood back.

Moses furiously asked Aaron how he had allowed this to happen.

"Oh Moses." he cried, "You were gone so long that the people thought all of you had died.

The people were in despair and confused and they did not know what to do so the old ways seemed good. Some of the people from the other nations and some who envied you persuaded them to bring all their gold jewelry that they had taken from Egypt and they would melt it down and make a golden calf. The goldsmiths were skilled and made it. The people had found some succulent plants nearby and had eaten of these. I think something in these plants clouded their minds. Hur tried to stop them and they killed him. Some said it was not a golden calf but it was a golden throne for God to sit upon and come to our aid. I knew that was wrong too, but I was powerless to stop them or I would have been slain also."

Moses saw that Aaron was impotent and the angry mob would not obey.

He raised his staff and called for all who stood for God to come to his side.   All the tribe of Levi did so as did many others.

Moses then approached the golden Calf, knocked it over and threw it into the fire.

Those that had called for them to make and worship it now were starting to attack Moses.

Those that stood with Moses drew their swords and they came to Moses side and fought. All that had opposed Moses were slain.

God was not appeased and threatened to destroy all the Israelites and start over with just Moses and Joshua and their families. Moses pleaded with God invoking the names of their ancestors, who had been looked upon with favor by God, Abraham, Isaac, Jacob, Rachel and Leah. God relented but did send a plague which sickened many. Miriam, Moses sister was so stricken and Moses prayed to God to save Miriam, and Miriam was healed.

Moses then did as God instructed and carved two tablets out of the stone.   He again climbed the mountain and again spent forty days and forty nights receiving God's laws. When he came down his face was radiant and he strode with pride and confidence. The Israelites received the laws and rejoiced.

I wondered what problems lay ahead.

CHAPTER 16

We remained for many days and nights in the Sinai wilderness by Mount Sinai. The smoke had cleared and sky was bright blue. With not a cloud in sight. Gone were the booming noises of thunder and the piercing blast of the ram's horn. Some bird's chirping was heard again. How pleasant it was.

A stream gurgling down the mountain formed into a clear, cool pond. We had a lasting supply of good water here. We continued to receive manna for our food. We had meat when a sheep or goat had been sacrificed or one may have perished from a fall or other natural cause. The shepherds tried to protect them but could not be everywhere the animals roamed.

Sometimes the hunters would bring back a gazelle. I would always get some good bones with plenty of meat on it, Yummy. I needed the meat as manna was not sufficient for a dog. There were shrubs and reeds growing by the pond which provided a food source for the animals. This was soon depleted and the herds of sheep and goats needed to constantly go further to find an area to graze. The goats were brought to the foothills of the mountain where there were shrubs that they happily munched down. The sheep were led to areas of grasses where they grazed. I had free time now so I went along with the shepherds to brush up on my super sheep-herding skills.

It was quiet in the camp but the people were very busy.

The young men and women were practicing with their bows, swords and spears in case we met hostile people when we moved onward. We hoped this would not be necessary.

Miriam and Zipporah had become good friends. They served as midwives, helping the women when they gave birth, and there were many births and babies. Other women also were taught these skills and became proficient midwives. The two organized and counseled the women. If one was troubled she would come to Miriam and Zipporah for advice. If a child became orphaned they would take it in with their own or find a family who would care for it. No child was abandoned.

Others were constructing a Tabernacle, or Meeting Tent, as God had directed Moses. When the people were slaves in Egypt they were forced to build temples for Pharaoh. Now they were free and rejoiced that they would build their own holy sanctuary, a place where God would appear to the chosen.

There were many who had held back their gold, horrified when the heretics had demanded it to build the golden calf. Horrified as the making of an idol violated the very teachings from the time of Abraham, and again stated by God. Now however they gladly brought gifts of gold, other precious metals, yarn made from the wool of their sheep, tanned rams hides, all with a sense of pride and achievement. Moses called upon one man, named Bezalel, a skilled craftsman, able to turn melted gold into beautiful cherubim or fine strands of woven gold.

I have to confess when I heard the name, Bezalel, it tickled my brain and when I repeated it to myself it tickled on my tongue. Bezalel, Bezalel, it sounds so funny. Moses however knew me and gave me a stern look, meaning, No!

The directions to erect the Meeting Tent were very specific and the people carefully followed these instructions as they proceeded. Who was permitted to enter the Tent was also narrowly defined and under what circumstances one may enter. Moses, Aaron and Aaron's sons, who were also priests, as was Aaron, were allowed. When Moses entered the Tent he would speak directly to God and when he came from the Tent his face would be shining.

God set down the laws and rules the people were to follow and Moses explained them carefully, and the people were glad and content as now they knew the laws they were to use as their standard.

Moses was very wise and told me that these rules set down by the creator were revolutionary as they forbid many customs commonly practiced throughout the lands. The idea of caring for all others, even those disabled or ill, humane treatment of animals, a day of rest and a prohibition of worshipping statues, idols, or images, set a higher standard for humanity. He said that thousands of years from now these commandments will be practiced by almost everyone as laws of their land. They won't even be aware that Gods laws changed the very accepted behaviors that were considered normal, such as beating slaves or, treating women as property.

The people pondered and studied these commandments to understand.

We had been encamped for many weeks. We were getting restless. The young men were looking for something to do. I came upon an old coconut that had fallen from a palm tree. We had brought it from the area near the Nile. I grabbed the coconut and dragged it towards the men. They laughed then one tried to grab it from me. He chased and I let go and he kicked the coconut along the sand until another man jumped up and he started kicking it. Others joined in then they decided to form two teams and try to kick the coconut across a line at the opposite end of the field. They started to keep score and they decided to call this game, "Soccer".

Then a day came when the shepherds came to Moses and advised that there was no more grazing land left in this area for our herds. Moses received the word that it was time for us to move towards our destination. We were excited to be moving forward but a bit sad as the area here had been a wonderful place for us.

Jethro, a high priest of Midian, and Moses' father-in-law, had come again to visit, bringing one of my pups, Number Four. Jethro knew the land and Moses persuaded Jethro to come with and help guide us.

Jethro, after much thought agreed. He was concerned about his wife and other daughters, and his many grandchildren, but he had many men who he knew would protect them. He also marveled at the miracles, the events and the giving of Gods laws, and was very curious as what was ahead. Jethro sent back some of his men to explain that he would visit with the Israelites for a while. Several of his young men agreed to come with us also.

What adventures and dangers were we to encounter?

CHAPTER 17

We again formed into the marching order and set out into the hot desert. The desert hot harsh sun bearing down upon us yet the desert was cold at night. The ground beneath us, hot sand, rocks that would cause one to trip and fall, strong winds that would blow stinging bits of sand into our faces. It was not easy, this nomadic, wandering life and the people were weary and wondering if they would all perish here. They began to doubt their faith in God.

We were within one day's journey to the Promised Land. Anticipation rose throughout the people. Moses sent men to scout the land that God had promised them. One man from each of the twelve tribes. These men were named Shammua, Joshua, Palti, Gaddiel, Gaddi, Ammiel, Sethur, Nahbi, Geuel, Shaphat and Caleb. What was the land and the inhabitants like? All eagerly awaited their reports.

We waited and waited and for forty days we waited and then I sniffed and saw someone in the distance and I knew it was them. I barked like crazy and ran in circles and the camp awoke and went running to welcome back the scouts and hear their news. The people were very excited but first they provided water and refreshments for the men. All the camp gathered to hear the reports. Some of the men showed them branches heavy with grapes and olives they had cut from the grape vines and olive trees in the land of Canaan. "It is a rich land of milk and honey", they told the masses, "but the people living there are fortified behind walls 30 to 50 feet high and 15 feet thick. The people there have powerful fighting forces. There are the tribes of Anakites, Amalekites, Hittites, Jebusites, Ammorites and Canaanites. We cannot beat them for they are more powerful than we."

The people reacted with fear and a terrible sense of depression. "Why did you bring us here only to die in the wilderness?" they cried.

Caleb rose to speak. "I have also seen this land and the people who live there. The land is good. The coastal plains have much water and very good soil. The central mountains are covered with forests for lumber and the valleys are among the very fertile. The lowland hills are ideal for vineyards and olive groves. There are also desert areas not suitable for farming. The people there are not giants but mere mortals. We will have God with us and we shall surely prevail."

Yet the people spent that night in mourning, believing all their effort to reach the Promised Land was in vain. They feared they would die in battle and their wives and children would be carried off and again made slaves. In the confusion and turmoil they gathered and were exceedingly angry with Moses.

Aaron rose demanding how these people could so quickly forget the miracles God had provided for them.

"Have faith in God!" he demanded.

But the people responded by threatening to stone Moses, Aaron and those who stood with them, even me. Moses, Aaron, Joshua and Caleb begged the people to listen to them.

"The land is a good, rich, fertile land, and God will provide the land for us and our children but you must have faith in God or he will not protect us."

Just then the presence of God appeared in the Tent of Meeting and spoke to Moses.

"Have I chosen the wrong people? Despite all I have done, all I have accomplished for them, they cry and lose faith at every hardship. Shall I strike them all with a deadly illness and start again with you few who remained steadfast in your faith?"

Moses had always been reluctant to speak, as he was embarrassed about his speech defect, but now he spoke eloquently with words that a poet would envy and God relented.

"I shall pardon but all who lost faith, all over the age of twenty, shall wander in the wilderness for many years and shall not enter the Promised Land."

Moses told the gathering of God's words. It was as a knife piercing the heart. They were overcome with grief and now the fear of powerful armies to overcome was replaced by the realization that they were so close but would never get to their longed-for destination. Early the next morning they rose and were determined to march to the land they so desired.

Moses warned them to cease telling them they would be defying God's words.

"We were wrong in fearing to enter the land and we must go there."

As a mob they moved towards the hills to enter the land.

Moses pleaded with them to stop as did Aaron and Joshua but there words were useless and not heeded.

There was no battle order as they took their swords and spears and approached the hills.

Joshua and his trained warriors stood with Moses, as did many others. They called for the mob to return but their shouts were in vain.

The Amalekites and Canaanites were waiting with their bows at the ready. As the mob ran up the hill they were met with a storm of arrows. Many of the mob fell. The enemy then came rushing towards them with spears pointed at their chests and impaled those of the front of the mob, then with swords and axes began viciously hacking at them. The mob of people were disorganized and without God's help were quickly beaten. They turned and ran back towards their camp, helping and carrying the wounded.

One of the men lay on the hillside, struggling to crawl back to us but was badly wounded and needed help. I and pup number four quickly jumped forward and ran to the hill to his side.

The enemy was laughing and thought we were wild dogs that had come to devour the wounded man. Pup number four and I bit and held onto his clothing and dragged him back to the camp.

The Amalekites shot arrows at us when they realized we were bringing him to safety but they all missed.

Joshua and his warriors formed a line of defense, with spears at the ready, and the enemy withdrew back to their hills.

We dragged the wounded man to the shade of a Tamarisk tree. He was sorely wounded and would not recover. His wife and children ran to his side. They were weeping.

"I wanted so badly to reach the Promised Land but I failed." He told them. "Now I have also defied God so my soul will not return to God's kingdom."

Joshua, overhearing the man's tragic lament, replied. "God is as a father, merciful and forgiving to all who pray to him and repent. Ask God to forgive."

The man did so, acknowledging that God is supreme and begging God to forgive him and to accept his soul.

A cloud appeared hovering over the man and a deep, resounding voice was heard. "I have pardoned."

The anguish on the man's face turned to a look of relief. "I have been forgiven and God has assured me that our children will arrive in the Promised Land." His eyes closed and he breathed no more.

CHAPTER 18

We were now destined to wander for years before entering the holy land. We again trudged through the hot desert, making camp when we found a suitable spot.

The people were downcast. They had been so close yet the actions of the many of the community led to punishment for all, even those who had obeyed.

Why are we penalized when we stood by God's words? Many asked themselves.

Aaron tried to find an answer. "Those in a community are responsible for one another.

When we did not speak out and persuade the others we failed in our responsibility. It is the same as seeing someone doing something wrong and failing to speak or act."

Some understood and accepted Aaron's reasoning.

Some did not. Some were envious of Moses and Aaron and began to question their authority.

Korah was one who began to speak against Moses. Two hundred and fifty men, some were leaders of their tribes, joined with Korah against Moses.

"You took us away from the land of milk and honey to perish here in the wilderness!" they accused Moses.

"Why do you act as if you are holier than we?" they demanded.

"I am only an instrument of God." Moses replied. "Tomorrow morning we shall gather and all shall pray and God shall answer to your complaints."

The following morning Moses, Aaron, Joshua, pup number four and me, and many, many others gathered on the side of the hill. Korah and his followers did not leave their tents to join Moses demonstrating their refusal to obey and their rejection of Moses. Moses prayed but God was angry that Korah and his followers disputed God's choice of Moses as a spokesman. God threatened to destroy all the Israelites.

Moses again pleaded, "When one man sins, will you destroy all the people?"

God relented and told Moses to have all the people stand away from the tents of Korah and his followers, and they did so.

A loud rumbling noise was heard, the ground shook, and Korah's tents, his followers, their wives and children fell into a fissure that had opened beneath their feet. Clouds of smoke, dust and flames rose from the fissure.

Those on the hillside ran back in terror fearing the opening would engulf them also.

The rumbling ceased and the cloud of smoke and dust died down. The people strained forward to see what had happened to Korah and all that had rebelled. .They were distressed that, though this group had rejected Moses, they were people they knew, some were friends and some even were relatives. Slowly survivors began to climb out of the hole. Women, clutching their children, followed by many of the men.

They were covered with dust and ashes. They had stared into the flames of God's wrath but God had spared them. All climbed out, except Korah. The leaders were chastened and vowed never, ever, to doubt the word of Moses again. One of the children, Samuel, was destined to be a prophet and the father of Saul, who became their King, but that is another story.

Why did God spare their lives? As a father disciplines but loves his children so did God punish to turn them away from evil. God would rather have those who repent become strong supporters rather than to have them perish.

So we wandered. The people had come so close to the Promised Land but were turned away and they were forlorn and sad. Most of their hopes and dreams were gone. Those who were over the age of twenty were now destined never to enter the Promised Land, to remain in the wilderness until the end of their days. The one remaining dream that kept them going was that their children, grandchildren and future generations would enter and thrive in the land that was denied to them. God had commanded the people to choose life, never death, so they trudged forward.

Moses told me that the average person, at that time, lived for about only twenty-seven years. Some lived to thirty-five or forty. Many passed away before age twenty-seven due to illness or injury. He said God had told him that hundreds of years into the future, with better health and diets, better knowledge about cleanliness and vaccinations preventing disease, people would live to ninety, one hundred or even one hundred and fifty years of age.

It was happening as we tried to survive in the desert. The harsh, arid, hot, unforgiving climate of the desert. Gradually many of the older people began to succumb including Moses' sister, Miriam.

Miriam who had followed Moses when as an infant he floated down the Nile in a basket. Miriam who had seen the Egyptian princess pull the basket from the Nile and it was Miriam who volunteered the services of her mother to wet nurse and care for the baby, Moses. Miriam who had grabbed her timbrel and led the women in dance and song as they praised God for the miracle of bringing them safely across the Sea of Reeds. Miriam, the ancestor of David, to be the Kings of Israel.

Moses was desolate. I wagged my tail and barked my friendly, "Hi, cheer up." bark, but it was better that I just sat next to him and he knew I was there.

God spoke to Moses to reassure him. "Miriam's name will forever be remembered for she was the one who called upon the people to praise their God and her dancing and songs shall be an inspiration to those who make music, forever." Miriam was buried at a placed called, Kadesh in the wilderness of Zin.

It was not all sad. The children grew to become teenagers, married and had children of their own.

The entire community joyously celebrated such weddings and especially the birth of the new babies.

These babies, born and playing as they grew, under the hot desert sun and climate, were a different breed. They were able to go long periods without water, grew lean and strong, agile and quick. They never knew slavery, only freedom.

CHAPTER 19

We were without water again, which is very serious in the hot desert. I tried but could not sniff any hint of water in the area. It was barren. Not a tree in sight. No clouds either. Just a broiling hot sun. We were at Kadesh in the wilderness of Zin.

The people again were quick to complain.

Maybe I should not have said "quick". They were depressed for being denied entry to the holy land.

They had glimpsed it then it was pulled away and they were told the older people would die in the wilderness, never enjoying the fruits of their efforts. Friends and relatives had passed away.

They were sad, exhausted, hot and angry. They turned their anger again towards Moses and Aaron.

"You have led us to this barren wilderness that has no trees, vineyards, grasses, just sand and rocks.

There is no shade. There is no water! Surely now we shall all perish here. We were better off as slaves.

Aaron turned to Moses and Aaron was angry and bewildered. "I cannot understand these people.

How can they ever prefer slavery to freedom?"

Moses thought for an answer. Moses had not tasted of slavery but he had sympathized with them and understood their plight. He stammered a bit. "Slavery is terrible but it is also security. You have your role. You know your daily tasks. Freedom is uncertain. It is unstructured. Yes, here we are free but we struggle with day to day existence. Yet would you rather be a slave or a free person? Would you choose to make your own choices and decisions recognizing that some choices will lead to negative consequences but some will be very rewarding?'

Moses and Aaron went to the Tent of the Meeting and prayed for an answer and for water. Moses was angry that the people continued to lack faith and turn against him. He was also still saddened at the death of his older sister, Miriam. She had been like a second mother to him.

Again God's voice appeared and was heard. They were told to call the people together. Moses would raise his staff and order a large boulder, near the tent, on a slight slope, to produce water. There will be sufficient water for the people, their flocks of sheep, coats, cattle and other animals. They called the people together. Moses was still fuming. I knew his temper and had tried many times to teach him to control it.

Moses raised his staff as God instructed but someone yelled to him, "There is no Sea of Reeds here for you to part.! It is water we need!"

Moses ordered the rock to yield water but nothing happened. It was totally quiet. The air was still and hot. Not a bird flying by or chirping. The people watched and hoped for water. Some dust rose by the rock and a few pebbles slid down the incline.

Again Moses told the rock to give water and still nothing.

The people now were grumbling.

I saw Moses face turn red. His arm muscles flexed.

"No." I softly growled. "Don't do it."

Instead of commanding the rock to produce water Moses hit the rock hard, twice with his staff.

I thought the staff would break in two.

I heard a groan from somewhere. The rock split in two and water came out as a torrent. It rushed down the slope and formed into a large pool of water.

The people rushed forward plunging into it drinking, cheering. They filled their water skins and then watered the animals. They joked and laughed as they splashed the water on one another quickly forgetting their despair.

God was not pleased. Moses was to command the rock, not strike it. The rock would have produced the water had Moses been patient. It was to be a sign to the people about the harmony between man and nature. Now Moses' action had demonstrated that mankind would force and take from nature and by doing so would eventually lead to harm for all.

The waters here became known as Meribah -"The waters of strife".

CHAPTER 20

We broke camp and again started marching towards our destination. We came to the border of the kingdom of Edom and we needed to cross. Moses sent a message to the King of Edom that we desired only to cross the land to arrive at our destination. We shall avoid your vineyards and fields and remain only on the road. If we drink your water we shall make payment.

The King refused and brought a large, well-armed force to the border.

We were prepared to do battle but Moses was unwilling.

"We have walked so far and for so long already. We can take a detour and walk a bit longer. I do not want our young to sacrifice their lives in battle when it can be avoided."

Mount Hor was ahead of us, on the boundary with Edom. Here, at the base of Mount Hor, Aaron had reached the end of his days.

We made camp.

Moses, Aaron, and Aaron's son, Eleazer, climbed to the top of the mountain. We watched them climb up. When they came down it was only Moses and Eleazer. The holy, priestly garments, worn by Aaron, were now on his son, Eleazer. We knew Aaron had been laid to rest on top of the mountain.

We would miss Aaron. He was our spiritual leader. He had performed many weddings, officiated at the naming of newborns, led prayers over those who had died, counseled and was a steadying influence. Aaron worked for peace. Peace between God and the Israelites. Peace between people. When two men had a conflict he would sit down with them to mediate and would talk to them until their problem was resolved and they would make peace with one another.

He was not perfect. He had erred in participating in the making of the golden calf. But all men make mistakes and Aaron's good deeds were weighed very heavily against his few mistakes.

Moses was again in despair. His children and grandchildren consoled him and they were a pleasure to him. For thirty days we mourned the loss of Aaron, then it was time for the living to get about their lives.

We moved forward.

Where would our fate take us?

CHAPTER 21

Now Pup number four had developed a close relationship with Joshua. Both were adventurous.

Pup told me that he had made Joshua his person.   I was pleased. Everyone needs friends.

Our march took us along the Negev. The Canaanites lived there. I was in the front with Moses when pup number four came racing to us from the rear. We had many, many people in the twelve tribes and the marching order had spread us so far apart we could not know what was happening in the rear. Pup number four was out of breathe, he had been running so hard and fast, that he needed a few moments.   Finally he let me know that the Canaanites had attacked us from the side. They were waiting in hiding for the scouts and overpowered them, taking them prisoners. They then attacked the column taking some more prisoners before they were beaten off.

We prayed that God would give us strength to beat the Canaanites and if we did we would raze their village to the ground as dust.

We were not a group of slaves, old and infirmed. That age group had passed during the long marches. We were a group of young, strong warriors who knew only freedom. We had sharpened our skills with bows, spears and swords. We were ready to do battle to defend ourselves.

Our scouts found the enemy village. They were celebrating. Joshua sent one group to the right of the village and one to the left. Our main group was ready at the center. The archers, many of them were our young women, were ready with their bows. Joshua had a small group approach the Canaanite's village. They were seen and the Canaanites poured from the village to attack.

Our small group retreated, leading them right towards our main force. The Canaanites continued to advance, unaware they were now in a trap. Now our main force was in front of them and we had two forces on each side. They were surrounded on three sides. Our archers sent off their arrows, quickly, rapidly, one arrow after another, many striking the Canaanites, piercing their light armor.

They stopped and looked around but there was no shelter or escape for them. Our warriors then attacked from three sides with sword, spear and axe. They were stunned by our ferocity and strength. Many were cut down. The remaining Canaanites fled into their village. We pursued them, cutting them down, then as we had promised God, we destroyed the village, grinding it down to dust. We found our prisoners that they had taken. They had tortured some and abused the women.

They had killed some for their amusement. We brought the wounded back to our camp where their wounds were tended.

We rested then moved forward again. We marched along the east side of the Dead Sea crossing over the Arnon River into the land of the Amorites. Several days we had marched and we were again in need of water. I sniffed around and came to a spot which I sensed held much water. I started to dig but Moses had me stop. All the tribal chieftains were called together and they started to dig a well, using their spears as shovels. Moses had them stop and all the Israelites sang a song to the well, The Song of the Sea", and the well filled with water. Was this the beginning of karaoke? We drank, filled our water skins, and the animals then drank until they were satisfied.

Moses sent a message to Sihon, King of the Amorites, that we only wished to pass through his land, would not bother vineyard or farm fields, and would pay for any water we use. But Sihon refused and assembled his fighting forces to attack us. The battle took place at Jahaz.

Our archers again were outstanding in our defeating them. We sent volley after volley and they had no defense. Our young, strong, battle-hardened warriors now sprung forward, running towards them with spears stretched forward but then stopped as we got close and hurled the spears with deadly accuracy.

We then were on them with swords and axes, cutting, hacking and driving them to the ground.

The land the Amorites had taken in battle, from the former king of Moab, we now took in our possession, just as Moab had taken it from the prior inhabitants. All the land of the Amorites became ours.

Had Sihon agreed to our request there would have been no battle. Had Sihon and the Amorites defeated us, there would have been no more Israelites. We won and seized the land as the gains of victory. Thus it had been for centuries.

Moses sent a group to investigate Jazer, north of the Dead Sea, where some Amorites still remained, and Jazer fell to us as we approached.

Og, the King of Bashan, learned that we were approaching and he feared us and was also enraged. He brought his military forces to Edrei, a large, potent force, but God told Moses to have no fear as we would defeat them as we had the Amorites.

Joshua followed the same battle plan and had a small force which retreated and drew the enemy into a trap where they were surrounded on three sides. Our archers again were accurate causing many casualties, confusion and panic among the enemy lines. Our warriors then attacked totally destroying the enemy, their king and his sons, until all were gone.

All the land where we had fought and defeated the enemy was taken as our possession.

We camped and rested tending to our wounded and regaining our strength.

We were on the boundary of the land of Moab and here things got strange.

CHAPTER 22

The King of Moab, named Balok son of Zippor, became convinced we were going to attack. We had made no such advances. We were only recuperating. Nevertheless Balok called his senior advisors together and expressed his fears that the Israelites would wipe them out, as a dog licks clean his bowl of food. (I only do that when it's really good food. Yummy.) Anyway Moses learned that he had sent messengers to a man called, Balaam, who lived near the Euphrates River at a point close to where it emptied into the Persian Gulf.

What was there about this man, Balaam? He was reported to be an Oracle, a man who could make prophecies. He could deliver curses or blessings and it was told that these all came to pass. If he made a curse over a tribe or group, everyone believed his curse would become real. That group would be inflicted with terrible happenings. If he made a blessing over a group, those people would receive good fortunes, abundant crops in their fields, happiness and prosperity.

"Oh come now." Moses, "I growled. "How can a curse do that?"

"It is what people want to believe. If Balaam curses us our people will lack confidence, they will become distracted and depressed, believing that what Balaam said will happen. We can tell them that he has no real power but they would not believe us." Moses replied.

Now Moses learned that Balaam had refused the messengers sent by King Balok so we were all very relieved. But then the messengers were sent back to Balaam, a large group of wealthy and important men, and they promised very rich rewards to him if he would come to Moab and place a curse on the Israelites.

Balaam had come to recognize in the one, supreme God, and he told the messengers he was only able to predict or say what words God put in his mouth but he would sleep that night and listen to what God might tell him.

That night he heard God telling him he may go with these men but he would only be able to say that which God wanted him to speak.

The next morning he agreed to go with the men. They saddled their horses or camels while Balaam had his two servants saddle his donkey. They ate a quick breakfast, drank plenty of water, as it would be dry and thirsty along the way, packed water skins full of water, food and other provisions and set off.

In the meantime an angel, a messenger from God, came to Moses and instructed him that I should go to the path that Balaam will be on and wait for him.

Moses so instructed me and urged me to be careful. We had hardly ever been apart. He also told me that the word "messenger" was the greek word for angel. I wondered how Moses had learned greek. Must have been when he lived in the Pharaoh's palace.

I climbed up the mountain and came to the path that Balaam would have to take. There I waited.

A bee buzzed around me by some small yellow flowers growing among the rocks and I watched the bee for a while. The some birds flew by, chirping and darting down to catch some flying insects. They were smart to stay away from the bee who would have stung them. I waited some more. Then the birds gave some chirping noises and flew away and I knew something was coming along the path.

The narrow mountain path, had a wall of boulders and rock rising on one side, and a slight slope of land filled with growing grape vines on the other side. The vineyard slanted downhill then there was a steep drop.

Along came Balaam mounted on his donkey with two assistants trudging along behind him. The several men from King Balok followed.

Balaam was rather pudgy, and his face was round. He had a turban on his head and wore a bright yellow and red robe and purple pantaloons. His hands held out to the side with the reins on one hand and a willow tree stick in the other. He was bouncing along on the donkey and seemed to be deep in thought. He appeared very comical.

The angel instructed me to jump out in front of the donkey and stop it. I did, growling menacingly.

The angel made a veil appear about me so only the donkey could see me. The donkey stopped abruptly and Balaam almost fell forward over its head. He jerked the reins sharply and the donkey veered to the left and smashed Balaam's leg between the panicked animal and the rock wall.

Balaam let out a yelp of pain and started beating the donkey with the willow stick. The donkey then tried to go forward but I blocked its path so it turned into the vineyard. Again Balaam whipped the donkey trying to get him back on the road but I blocked its path. I was angry that Balaam mistreated hat poor donkey. It wasn't the donkeys fault. The donkey now had nowhere to go so it simply lay down. Balaam was embarrassed that his assistants and the men from Moan thought he was not able to control a donkey.

The donkey opened its mouth to bray and the angel spoke but the words seemed to come from the donkey.

"Why are you beating me? Haven't I carried you for years without a problem? Can't you see the path is blocked?"

The other men had seen neither me nor the angel and heard nothing.

"What, a talking donkey?" said Balaam. "I had seen in the future a talking donkey in a movie with an Ogre, but that was make believe."

Then the angel lifted the veil but only as far as Balaam could see. He made me appear to look like the angel". Now Balaam saw what he thought was an angel of God blocking his path and he understood the donkey was not at fault.

"I am sorry donkey." He said. Now this the others heard and looked at one another quizzically.

Balaam was shocked to see the angel and ask what the angel wanted of him.

I replied, actually it was the angel speaking through me. "You are to go with these men but you may say only that which God directs you to speak."

Balaam said he would, that he always only spoke the words which God put into his mouth.

The angel left. The men suddenly saw me and asked where did that dog come from?

They shoould have said, "Where did that handsome, strong, dog come from?

Anyway it was the time for me to leave and quickly I did.

I scooted down the mountain. When I got back to the camp I let Moses know what had happened.

He was sorry he had not been there to see it.

Balok, the King, came out to greet Balaam, and he asked him to put a horrible, terrible curse on the Israelites. Balaam said I can only utter the words God puts into my mouth.

Balok, along with Balaam and the dignitaries and wealthy men form Moab, went to the top of a high hill.

They built an alter and Balaam made a sacrifice to God.

There, atop the hill, with the dignitaries from Moab alongside, and the Israelites in the valley below, Balaam stretched his arms out in front, palms downward. As Balaam prepared to speak all sounds ceased. Not a bird chirped, neither a goat bleated nor did a donkey bray. Even the dripping noise of slow drops of water from a crevice between two rocks had halted.

Balaam spoke. His voice was deep and resonated throughout the surrounding hills.

In the valley below the Israelites had all stopped and stared at the figure of Balaam atop the hill.

Balaam's curse was considered powerful and the people were nervous.

"I come to foresee the doom of the Israelites but God has not doomed. I see them from the hilltop and they shall be as numerous as the dusts of a sand storm. May their God be mine. May my destiny be as great as their destiny."

Balok stood open-mouthed in shock.

"You were to place a curse on them. Instead you placed a blessing. What have you done?"

Balok's dignitaries stood in disbelief, muttering angrily amongst themselves, casting outraged looks at Balaam, while below the Israelites were relieved and jubilant.

"I am but a servant of God and may only speak that which God directs me to say."

"Come," said Balok, "Let us go to a different location. Perhaps from there you will successfully damn them."

Balok, Balaam, the dignitaries mounted upon their donkeys or horses and moved to another spot on a second hilltop. Below the Israelites looked on and listened intently.

Again Balaam raised his arms and prepared to place a curse on the Israelites. Again all movement paused waiting for his pronouncement. Not a peep was heard.

He spoke and his rich voice was rolled like thunder through the hills.

"No harm is in sight for the descendants of Jacob for God has blessed them. God freed them from slavery and is in their midst. They shall spring forward as a lion, devouring all in its path."

Balok jumped up and down crying, "No, no, no! You were to curse, not bless."

"I can only say what words God places in my mind." Balaam replied.

Balaam's donkey made a braying sound which sounded lot like laughter.

"Don't curse! Don't bless! Don't say anything!" Balok demanded, stamping his foot on the ground.

"Wait! We shall go to another spot, one with some shade and I will get you some water for your thirst and this time you will be able to place the curse."

They moved again to another hill and there, halfway up the hill, under the shade of a desert tree, Balaam drank, cleared his throat and prepared again to curse the Israelites, who were now waving and laughing at them.

He looked down upon the Israelites camp, seeing families of men, women and children, hundreds and thousands. The tents were arranged orderly and in a way where the entrances were shielded from the nearby tents to respect each other's privacy. He saw a holiness around them for God was with them.

He spoke marveling at this impressive sight of thousands of tents. "I cannot curse that which God protects." he stated. "I see a people that shall crush their enemies and they shall thrive as long as their God is with them. Those who curse you shall be cursed." Were his final words.

Balok threw himself on the ground, beating it with his fists and kicking with his feet.

"No, no, no!" he screamed. "You were to curse, not bless. Go, go! No reward for you!"

I told your messengers I am only a tool used as God sees fit. I am only able to foresee that which God permits and say that which God allows. Before I take leave let me tell you that which I have been granted to see.

"The Israelites shall be as a meteor, smashing those in its path as God wills. A light shall shine from them for the other nations, yet they shall remain a nation apart. They shall suffer if they turn away from God. Thrice they shall so suffer but shall rebound with a renewed faith in God, stronger each time than before."

And Balaam left Balok and began his journey home.

In the valley below we were joyful. We rested, recuperated, and prepared to move on.

CHAPTER 23

I liked Phinehas. He always had time to rub my belly and often had a juicy bone to throw to me.

He was the son of Eleazer, the son of Aaron, the priest. He was well-respected in our community.

Oh, he was black. No one cared about that. Look at my pups. Some had yellow coats, some tawny, some black, some white, some mixed. It didn't change who they were. All were cute pups and were growing up to be strong, proud dogs. The color on the outside doesn't change who you are inside. I make mention of it only as most of the Israelites were white but there were some who were black. Indeed Moses had taken a second wife, a Cushite woman who was also black.

We were camping in an area north of the Dead Sea, an area inhabited by the Moabites and Midianites. Their women dressed in a way to attract and seduce the Israelite men. They worshipped the Moabite god, Baal. Some of our men drew close to the Moabite and Midianite women and they too started to turn towards Baal.

The tribal chiefs called a meeting because of this irreverent behavior but one man, Zimri, in complete defiance and in a disreputable act degrading to God brought his Midianite woman into the meeting tent. This was so offensive to man and God that we feared God would turn his wrath on the entire community.

Phinehas acted quickly. He was enraged. He drew his sword and forced Zimri and the woman out of the tent and brought them to the boundaries of our camp. There he exiled them from the Israelite community forever.

If they attempted to return the guards would bar their way. If seen we would shun them by turning our faces away. Zimri was doomed to never again see his parents, brothers and sisters, his wife and their children. He had brought shame and disgrace upon himself forever.

An illness had started, we believe it had been spread from the Moabite women to our men who, in turn, infected their wives. We prayed to God to heal those who were ill. Because of Phinehas's action God heeded our prayers and the illness stopped.

As Phinehas had shown his strong faith God elevated him to the priesthood. There was one problem. He could not sing any of the hymns or prayers and only spoke the words. It seemed he was unable to carry a tune and his voice was not harmonic but his voice resonated deeply and when he spoke all listened.

Phinehas was grateful that God had allowed him to become a priest and he celebrated and got me some extra juicy bones.

Moses was instructed to have a census taken and a count was made of all the male warriors of eleven of the tribes. The men of the twelfth tribe of Levi were not counted as fighting men as they were all priests. It was also decreed that the laws of inheritance were from father to son.

The women who had fought valiantly as our archers, and were impor-tant in turning the battles into our victories appealed to Moses that the lines of inheritance should also be from mother to daughter.

This also was so decreed.

Moses knew his lifetime was coming to an end. He was very tired. We had walked long distances for many, many months. He had accom-plished wonders and seen great things. He could not leave the people without direction.

God instructed him to select Joshua, the son of Nun. God told Moses that as a flock needs a shepherd so the people needed a strong leader.

I went looking for Joshua and found Pup Number four and Joshua playing. Joshua would toss a bone that pup would run for, bring it back, then Joshua would try to grab it from pup's mouth while pup would growl and keep his teeth clenched tightly on the bone. They both were having fun.

I barked until Joshua understood that I needed to follow him I brought him, and pup number four, back to Moses.

The entire Israelite community, all the men, women and children, and those who were not Israelites but journeyed with them, assembled. On the side of a hill, elevated, so all could see, Moses placed his hands on Joshua's head, and blessed him and handed to Joshua, so all could see, the staff of leadership and all knew that Joshua was to be our next leader, and we saw it was so.

CHAPTER 24

The following morning Moses listened to the voice of God and called a gathering to report God's instructions.

"The Midianite's behavior, attempting to seduce our young men to worship the Midian idol, was hateful to God and therefore God has decreed that we are to go forth and wipe out this scourge. Leave none who participated in this seduction alive!"

Again we prepared for battle.

One thousand warriors from each tribe were chosen.

Phinehas accompanied the warriors ready to sound the trumpet.

Moses had a special task for me and pup number four. He sent us, along with one hundred men, the night before the battle, to a hillside overlooking the Midianites camp. The men spread out on the side and top of the hill and each built a campfire. The Midianites saw one hundred campfires and believed that the Israelite army was on the hill. They turned their forces to withstand an Israelite assault from the hill and spent the night building a protective mound of logs, sand, rocks and soil. Long poles, with their end sharpened, were jammed into the base of this mound, sharpened end pointed outward, to impale men and horses that night charge against them. Behind the mound the Midianites were protected from our arrows. They would launch their arrows over the mound where they would fall upon our warriors as they advanced.

It was still dark but starting to get light. Each of the one hundred then lit a torch and started moving down the hill. The enemy thought all our army was now coming towards them. I and pup number four, I wish

I remembered his name instead of just number four, each had the handle of a burning torch placed in our mouth and we held on securely. We had a fear of fire so this was difficult for us. On a cold night I like to lay next to a roaring fire to warm up but I always have a healthy respect for flames. Now we had a job to do so we overcame our fears.

We ran along the hill with our torches and to the enemy it must have looked like our men were now starting to attack them from their right. The Midianites quickly now started to build a barrier on their right side, dragging over some logs, throwing on rocks, sand in a desperate, exhausting effort.

Meanwhile the main body of our warriors were sitting on horses prepared to charge. As the dawn light rose enough, so we could see, Phinehas blew on the ram's horn giving a loud blast. The archers fired a volley of arrows, one after another, again and again, and we urged our horses forward and charged.

The Midianite men were totally confused. They had seen what they thought was our army on the hill but now a horn blast from their rear, arrows striking left and right, men falling, a thunder from the galloping hoofs of thousands of horses, and the sudden realization that they were being attacked from their rear. They had prepared for a frontal assault and it was too late for them to shift their defenses. Our army was on them now, slashing with sword, stabbing with spear, men were falling and were trampled by the oncoming horses. They were disorganized, exhausted from trying to throw together the barriers, panicked and quickly destroyed by our onslaught. It was a decisive victory. All the Midianite warriors had fallen and our losses were very slight.

The five Kings of Midian were slain as were the women who had drawn God's wrath. The women, too young to have participated were seized and joined our ranks. Huge amounts of gold, jewelry, copper pendants, and other precious material was taken as booty. Thousands of cattle, oxen, sheep, goats and donkeys were also taken as spoils for the victors.

The herds of livestock were apportioned amongst the twelve tribes, allowing a portion for the priests and for sacrifice to God, who was with us. The gold and other precious materials were also divided fairly between all.

After the battle it was time to rest and recover.

Moses was troubled as some of the slain women had been pregnant. He brought the question to God of the unborn babies who had committed no offense.

"All life is precious to me," said God, "but what is life? If a man casts his sperm upon the ground was that life? If a woman's egg falls from her body, was that life? When I created Adam I passed over his body and gave the breath of life into his nostrils. With such breath I gave Adam his soul. Human life requires a soul or it is not life."

The land we were now in was fertile and able to support the cattle, sheep, and other animals, and to grow crops. Our herds had grown significantly with the addition of the livestock we had taken.

The tribes of Gad, Reuben, and many of Manasseh, now desired to remain and build their homes and towns and cities in this land. The land was east of the Jordan and I learned that at some distant time in the future it would be called, Transjordan. Ammon was the capitol city.

Moses was distressed that these tribes would make this area their home and not proceed to the land God had outlined as the Promised Land, the other side of the Jordan.

The tribes swore to Moses that they would stand with the other Israelites, sending their warriors to the very forefront of our further battles as we moved into the lands promised by God, and Moses agreed and was at peace.

The people of the tribes of Gad, Reuben and many of the tribe of Manasseh thereby established their homes and towns on the land east of the Jordan where they tended their flocks and began their vineyards and it was good.

CHAPTER 25

When a man believes he is reaching the end of his days he feels a need to communicate to his children certain vital information. Such might include the location of special documents, a hiding place for valuables, his family history and perhaps a favorite fishing or hunting spot. Such it was with Moses. He called the people together and reviewed the wondrous events that had occurred; the plagues brought upon the Egyptian people leading to their releasing the Israelites from bondage; the crossing of the Sea of Reeds; manna that fed them and drinking water provided from striking rocks; the receipt of the Ten Commandments and all of Gods laws; the defeats of their enemies and the fertile land they had received and the Promised Land to come. Moses also pointed out their transgressions and the punishments of those who transgressed. He urged us to live a righteous life.

"God has been with us, showing the way, leading us through the wilderness, defeating our enemies, but if we sin against God we will surely fail. Others, in the future, will try to follow our route through the desert, but they be unable to find God's water and will turn back or perish."

I have to admit that I, a really special dog, had a pretty good sniffer for finding water but God had provided where I found nothing. If God had not provided the water, well I hate to think about what would have happened.

Moses set down in writing the laws he had received. He tried to clarify a code of conduct, of fair and reasonable disciplines for transgressions where the punishment could not be greater than the harmful act. If a person caused another the loss of a hand he, or she, could not suffer greater than the loss of his or her, hand. However the punishment need not be as severe, especially if the circumstances showed the act was an accident.

As you recall an angel had appeared and spoken to me when I blocked Balaam's donkey.

The angel had appeared once or twice again and in chatting with me told me about a man, who would live in centuries to come, and was a chief of a family tribe. The tribe was called Family of Maphea. The man, he was called Don, was at the end of his life. He and his son had a plan to avenge actions that had been taken against their family. Don went over the plan repeatedly with his son, wanting to be assured that it would be done correctly.

I think it was this way now with Moses. Three times he called an assembly of all the people to review their wanderings and urge them to choose life by following God's laws. As a father worries about his children so Moses was concerned about their fate after he would be gone.

CHAPTER 26

Joshua, now the leader, selected two young men and sent them across the Jordan River to spy upon Jericho. The two, Gad and Ishi, left their camp in the evening. It was still and quiet.

The torchlights of the city could be seen in the distance. The Jordan River was high and moving swiftly. They slipped in to the water. It was cold. They waded then swam across. Their clothing was soaked but was drying out as they lay in hiding near the city. They saw that the city was surrounded by a massive wall built of boulders piled one on top of another, with a second layer behind the first. Sand and small rocks filled the spaces between the boulders. The wall was fifteen feet high. Behind it a series of platforms had been built providing protection for the defenders against arrows, spears, or other missiles hurled by attackers. The defenders could shoot their arrows in an arc, from behind the wall, which would land upon approaching warriors.

The two men hid until dawn, then mingled with a group of traders approaching the gates of the city. The traders intended to sell their wares at the market. Gad and Ishi had nothing to sell and others grew suspicious of them. Word was sent to the King.

The spies quickly learned that the population was in great fear of the nearby Israelite army.

The King however had learned that two spies had come to the city and sent armed men to find them.

Anyone giving the spies aid would be executed.

Gad and Ishi saw the armed men searching and tried to find a place to hide. They came upon a very beautiful woman who was selling her wares. Her name was Rahab. She saw their clothing and mannerisms were different and realized these were the two spies the King had ordered his men to find.

Rahab told the two to go with her to her home. Her home was part of the wall. It had actually been built into the wall which served as the back of her home. There was one large room which was her kitchen, and a ladder leading to a floor above the top of the wall. Here was a bedroom. The bedroom had a window just above the wall.

Knowing she and her family would be killed if she was found giving shelter to these spies, she nevertheless took them in. She led them up the ladder to the top floor, where they then climbed to the reed- covered roof of her home and hid under a stack of reeds. Soon there was a pounding on the front door panel and Rahab opened it to find the Kings men there. They demanded to enter telling her the spies were seen going into the home.

"They forced their way in then saw you approaching and climbed out from the window above. If you go after them you will overtake them before they reach the river."

The men immediately rode off but had to ride through the city to reach the gate. They pushed their horses along the plain heading towards the river but found no one. They continued searching along the river bank.

Rahab called the two men to climb back down. She told them we had heard how your God freed your people from slaves of the Pharaoh, how God's power divided the Sea of Reeds then closed over Pharaoh's army. How the Israelites have been as a tornado destroying all enemies in its path. "We know that you will conquer this land because your God is mighty, above all. I beg you, since I have protected you, that your men will spare the lives of my parents and family. I seek to join the Israelites and worship your God."

Gad and Ishi pledged that she would be protected. "Tie a red cord to your window so we shall know that this home is to be spared and we promise that all who are inside it shall live."

Rahab tied one end of a rope to a strong wooden post throwing the rope out the window.

"Hide in the hills for three days so you will not be found, for if you are you shall surely be put to death along with me and my family."

They promised they would do as she asked and they climbed down the rope, concealed themselves behind a shrub or tree if anyone approached and worked their way to the hills. For three days and nights they remained in hiding, then the way was clear and they returned to the Jordan, swam back, and rejoined their camp.

They reported to Joshua what they had seen and learned and of the beautiful woman, Rahab, who had risked her life to help them. Joshua was troubled about the strength of the wall around Jericho and intrigued about the woman, Rahab.

CHAPTER 27

God spoke to Moses telling him to climb to the peak of Mount Nebo, in the land of Moab, facing Jericho.

Moses and I climbed the mountain. There, under the shade of a Cedar tree, Moses sat in the shade and rested. His time was coming to an end. He had brought food and water.

I had been given an assignment so I had to leave but I would return to be with him. He understood.

I was sad that he would be alone until my return but he assured me he would not be alone. From his perch on the mountain top he could see for miles and the drama that was to take place.

Now God was communicating with Joshua and instructed him on the attack and what would be the fall of Jericho.

We started the next morning. We had first to cross the Jordan River. The river, at this time of the year, was full, flowing rapidly. We could hear the gurgling, splashing noises and as we looked at the rushing, white water, we wondered how we would all get across. The priests, carrying the Holy Ark, started to cross and the water ceased to flow. It was another wonderful act by God. The river bottom was now dry and we crossed over safely. When our entire camp had crossed the waters flowed again.

We made our camp in sight of the walls of Jericho.

Three days we rested and prepared to do battle. Prayers were offered for the warrior's safety.

The strong gates of the city had been closed, not a soul entering or leaving. They saw our camps and knew we would be coming.

The next morning, as the Sun's rays began to lighten the scene Joshua gave us marching orders.

The fighting men of the tribes of Gad, Reuben and half of the tribe of Manasseh, moved first and behind them the priests carried the Holy Ark. Other fighters marched behind the ark. Seven priests carried ram's horns next to the ark. They approached the city walls and we knew the people inside were watching. The procession marched around the city, circling it while the priests blew the piercing, reverberating blasts of the ram's horn. Birds took to the air, frightened by the loud trumpets.

Meanwhile, while everyone watched the marchers and the priests, I and Pup number four, casually made our way to the wall, as if we were stray dogs searching for food.

The wall was huge made up of large boulders piled on top of one another on a sandy, rocky base.

Dogs are good diggers, and pup and I are among the best. We found a good spot and started digging.

No one saw us or if they did paid no attention. No big deal about two dogs digging. While the men were marching, the priests were blowing, we were digging. We dug and dug, deep down, tunneling under some of the large boulders.

After circling the city once our men marched back to their camp. Pup and I dug until it got dark then we returned to the camp for needed water, food and rest.

I hoped Moses was alright and I looked up towards the top of Mount Nebo and I thought I saw a small campfire there.

The next day, at dawn, the fighting men again marched in front of and behind the Ark which the priests carried. Seven priests again blew on their Ram's horns the loud, piercing sounds and again birds were startled and flew off in the sky above. The procession again circled around the city while those inside and on the wall watched. Some of the Jericho armed men, who were watching from atop the wall started to jeer and call out insults, as if we were afraid of them. Our men did not reply.

Again, pup and I, sauntered over to the wall and no one paid us any notice. We went to the same spot and started digging again, making deeper the tunnels and undercutting the boulders. We worked all day and returned to our camp in the evening.

This went on every day for the next four days. Now the people of Jericho all stood on the top of the wall laughing at us, yelling insults, vile names, and even tossing stones and garbage towards us. Our men were out of range of the things they threw but we could hear them. No one replied. Our day would soon come.

Pup and I kept digging but were careful not to dig near the window with the red cord.

On the seventh day we rose and saw an eagle circling above. It was a good omen. The morning was cool though the day would warm up. Our men again marched towards the city, the priests carrying the Holy Ark, and the seven priests sounding on their trumpets. Our archers also moved with the men then took up firing positions facing the wall. Joshua had told us this time we would all join the sounds of the Ram's horn by yelling our loudest. We circled the city, seven times, ignoring the people, on top of the wall, who thought we feared to attack them and continued calling out insults. On Joshua's signal the priests raised their trumpets and blew the loudest, longest, most piercing blasts yet, and now our men all yelled as loud as they could, while Pup and I were howling as loud as we could. The sound was deafening

The boulders began to tremble and teeter, where we had dug out the earth from around their Base, and suddenly with a roaring, crashing noise one boulder, then another started to shift and roll over, and it was as a set of dominoes with each knocking down another. The wall started to collapse in the spot we had dug out, then the sections next to it began to collapse until the entire wall had fallen apart. Clouds of dust rose from the wall and those who had been standing on top had fallen among the boulders and been crushed. Our archers fired their arrows and our men charged in. The defenders tried to beat us back, but with our shields blocking their swords, our spears finding their targets, and our sharp, slashing swords, the enemy was soon destroyed.

Our men had been instructed to avoid the home where a red cord hung from the window and they were careful to do so. We kept our promise to Rahab and she, her parents, family, and all in her home were spared. Joshua wanted to meet with this heroic woman to thank her for her help and it was said he was smitten by her beauty. Rahab was welcomed by the Israelites.

Was there to be a marriage between Joshua and Rahab? I wondered?

We now were in the Promised Land and now there would be further tribes we would have to battle and defeat, but these were smaller groups and God was with us. The Promised Land which the Israelites had reached after arduous struggles through the wilderness, had fought for valiantly, suffering losses but triumphing over their enemies, the Promised Land wondrous as God had told them. Many had sacrificed their lives in our struggles.

The land would be our homeland and we would farm it, irrigate it, turn wasteland into lush farmland, grow vineyards and fig trees, tend our flocks and thrive.

Of the people we defeated and claimed the land for our own, such had been the accepted custom for centuries. These people had conquered that land from those there before them who had seized it from those before them. The people we displaced migrated to other areas or many joined with us.

There was intermarriage and we accepted these people into our faith. As Moses himself had intermarried we had no problem with it.

What of Moses?

I raced back to return to Moses. Was he okay?

CHAPTER 28

Up Mount Nebo I dashed and to my relief Moses was there, waiting my return. I jumped on him and he hugged and petted me. He had watched and seen the fall of Jericho, amazed as the walls had fallen, but knowing it was with God's help.

He had not eaten too much. He had been busy.

Moses had brought with him several rolls of parchment and a box made of cedar. To my surprise he had inscribed on the parchment the story of my journey with him, from the time I had first seen him by Jethro's well, up to the falling of the wall. He added some markings on the parchments, rolled them up, and placed them in the cedar wood box.

We climbed part way down the mountain to a small cave and there we placed the box in the cave and pushed some rocks to cover the entrance.

"Someday, someone will find this and know the story of our journey together." He said.

We climbed back up to the top by the cedar tree where, exhausted, Moses sat and rested.

He called out to God.

"My God, you have done wonderful miracles for my people and I have tried to be a good leader and done what you required of me. God, I can see the Promised Land from here but cannot touch or feel it. God, I regret any mistakes I have made. Might not you reconsider and allow me to bring my tired body there, to lie upon its soil?"

God replied. "Moses, I explained to you by the burning bush that yours would be a difficult task.

This is the most difficult part. You are not to lie in the soil of the Promised Land for your grave would become a monument where the people would come to pray. They would direct their prayers not to God but to you. There is but one God and there shall be no idols, graven images, statues or likenesses that people might worship. You are but human and mistakes you made are forgiven.

It is not that which you did that prevents your entering. It is that you were too great."

Moses sadly understood.

"God, why was it necessary for you to be so hard on our people? They, as I, made mistakes for we are only mortals and it is you who are perfect."

"They are the first generation and as goes the first so much the example must be made. Should I have allowed this generation to slide away from the laws commanded, future generations would move away even further. I do not expect every commandment to be followed. I have given you an outline to govern behavior and these may be compacted into a basic law; to give others the same respect you would have them give you. The people are to read and understand that this is the basis of the law and if they behave justly I would be satisfied."

"God, we are to treat people with justice yet you commanded that we wipe out a whole group of people who had brought upon themselves your wrath. Why, God, so harsh?"

"It is the story of a fisherman. Every time he tells of the fish he caught the fish grows larger and larger.

The history of the people's release from bondage, escape across the Sea of Reeds, their hardships and triumphs in the desert wilderness, their victories and defeats, and their sacrifices and fight to win the land that they shall occupy, shall be told and retold, from generation to generation until it shall be transcribed, and with each telling and retelling the numbers will grow and grow and grow even larger. The death of one shall become exaggerated into the death of one thousand then into ten thousand. My creations are precious to me! Every life is precious. Every tree, animal, fish, and person are all precious to me.

God allowed Moses a vision of the future. He saw the land now developed by the Israelites. Barren land was now turned into orchards and farms. Cities were built. The people were strong and resolute. They had developed ways to minimize the use of water which they were teaching throughout the world. New technologies were being developed. Their armies were strong also and Moses was pleased.

"Now you must be tired and it is time to sleep."

So Moses rested against the cedar tree, my head resting on his lap. He closed his eyes. His breathing was slower. I also was very tired. We had a long journey together.

Then my friend, the angel, who had appeared with Balaam's donkey, again appeared.

The angel placed his hand over Moses' mouth and with Moses' last breath the angel reclaimed Moses' soul which was now to return to God.

The Angel smiled at me and I slept.

The End

Yet this is the end of one story but only the beginning as the Israelites journeys continued. The story of David defeating Goliath, of the Maccabees victory over evil, of the wealth of Solomon and so much more await you. Read about these and so much more in the Bible.